Bi

Brooklyn

A Novella

Brothers
of
Brooklyn

A Novella

Gary M. Cianci

Published by Marblestone Press
eBook ISBN: 978-1-7379870-0-0
Paperback ISBN: 978-1-7379870-0-0

Brothers of Brooklyn
Cover Design by Nick Mazzo, nmazzo86@gmail.com

DEDICATION

For my father, Dominick

ACKNOWLEDGEMENTS

Special thanks to my daughter, Suzanna, for her expert computer skills and relentless research. Without her at my side, this story does not get written.

Thanks to Henry Stewart, a writer and historian, for opening doors to my research. He showed me critical tools that became the basis of my work.

Appreciate early readers Carla Price, who especially helped my direction, and Toni Sternberg.

Janet Fix, *thewordverve inc.*, set a tone to the storytelling with her editing and put style and color into the work.

Nick Mazzo created eye-catching cover art with astute attention to detail.

Angie Lovell, *Beech House Books*, guided the publishing process, offering a turnkey solution that was friendly and stress-free.

Thanks to my wife, Anna Patricia, and daughter, Julianne, for listening and motivating me as I told the book's stories out loud, the process for my writing.

Special thanks to our family dog, Minnie, for faithfully staying by me while I wrote this book.

For James—

"Like the metamorphosis of caterpillars changing to butterflies, the generation of a family with a shadowy side can transform. Then, passing into light, the next generation and its descendants will be free from the past to do good."

ONE

Behind the Eight Ball

Michael Cimino set his ancient fedora on the scarred-up wooden desk and blew out a long stream of cigar smoke. He stared at the mass of papers attesting to his family's dark past and wondered how much more there was to learn. An investigative reporter for a good part of his life, he now found himself investigating his own roots.

And it was as thrilling as it was disturbing.

~~~

The apparent murder of his grandfather, Vincenzo James "Jimmy" Cimino, was the consequence of a double-double cross—and his shooter had given him no way out. An archived newspaper article in the storied *Brooklyn Daily Flyer* reported that Jimmy was killed gangland-style in a poolroom in Gravesend, Brooklyn. That was on December 1, 1931; he was just twenty-six years old. The paradox is that Michael, part of the family's fourth generation living in America, had been brought up to be a good citizen. No crime, no Mafia, no gangs. A clean life, really. The only time he got involved in illegal shenanigans was when he was reporting on them. And that was decades ago.

Now sixty-seven years old, Michael knew that his family history was complicated. And that his father, Nicky Cimino, had broken away from the violence that haunted his past. Nicky had grown up without his father—and that absence, though a loss, had shaped his character for the better.

Not so for Jimmy, who reportedly paid the ultimate price. The location of his suspected killing, Gravesend, seemed grimly ironic. And the year of this attack on his life—1931—was a clue to his mysterious disappearance.

As Michael grew up, he'd heard hints and seen subtle gestures referring to the death of his grandfather. He'd always suspected these murmurings harbored something more sinister.

In the middle of 2017, he would begin to research his family's past in earnest and through any means possible.

The impetus for Michael's obsessive research was the *Brooklyn Daily Flyer* story. First, just keying in a combination of names on the internet with mild curiosity, he had discovered the news that described a young man with a pistol in each hand entering the poolroom. His grandfather, holding a pool cue and chewing on a toothpick, was about to make a shot.

"Jimmy," the gunman said, gesturing with one of his pistols, "get over there against the wall."

Jimmy hesitated but did not draw his 38-caliber revolver. Friends who had witnessed the shooting told the *Flyer* they had questioned his reluctance. "Jimmy always carried," they said, "and was quick to pull a trigger." But hell, the guy had two pistols pointed at him. Still, Jimmy reportedly did not move from the pool table. Instead, he leaned against it and shrugged. "You can say what you gotta say to me right here."

The gunman, about the same age as Jimmy, said

not a word. Rather, he fired a total of six shots, with one of the bullets reportedly piercing Jimmy's heart.

Visualizing the crime scene, Michael imagined Jimmy's blood spraying onto the green cloth of the billiard table, illuminated by overhead lamps. His blood, in a pool, was slowly dripping into the corner pocket. Michael's visualization contrasted his grand-father's red blood against the green cloth, causing him to think about how the holiday colors might have reminded surviving family members of a dispirited Christmas season for years to come.

The story reported this two-fisted gunman "fled in a black coupe." Then a crew of men, who had been shooting pool with Jimmy, carried his body to a fish-delivery wagon and drove off, ultimately to nowhere. The article ended by reporting on an anonymous phone call made to the old Coney Island Hospital— these yellow brick buildings have remained behind two white towers, which house the newer hospital fa-cility that later opened in 1954. According to the story, a call was made to alert the hospital about re-covering the truck and body, where both were aban-doned a mile away from the poolroom. Police believed the men first wanted to drive to the hospital but quickly got cold feet. Speculating on the men freezing up, Michael figured *they'd suddenly feared having to step forward as witnesses and being impli-cated in some way.*

For close to sixty years, Michael Cimino had never known whether his grandfather had been bur-ied or cremated. Nobody in his family would talk about it freely, even when questioned. They'd just shrug and mumble or divert his attention. It seemed to Michael as if Jimmy Cimino's body had vanished without a trace.

For all the former reporter's life, he didn't even know his grandfather's face. But about six months after discovering the *Brooklyn Daily Flyer* story online, a family member finally shared with him a wedding photograph of his grandfather that had been passed down through the generations. Seeing his grandfather's face for the first time greatly moved him emotionally, even feeling a little ghostly. Family members who later saw this photograph claimed the two men closely resembled each other. Michael even wondered if his grandfather had the same hazel-colored eyes like him. A rare color, Michael's eyes combined brown, green, amber, and flecks of blue—and changed colors, depending on what he wore and the kind of lighting around him. The hazel color may have skipped a generation like the genetics of the two men's other facial features. But the black-and-white photograph, of course, did not show color so he could not know for sure. Still, because of their strong likeness, Michael instantly felt a connection to his grandfather and the drive to know more about his ancestors' hidden past. Michael picked up the photograph now, viewing it with his practiced eye for details. His grandfather was Hollywood handsome. He had eyes shaped like almonds, high cheekbones, a sharp nose, and a well-defined mouth. His lips were full, with a slight quirk to one side that had surely caught the eye of many ladies. His jawline was squared off, evoking a sense of confidence, and his dark hair was slicked-back, receding slightly at his temples.

Tossing the photograph back onto his desk and chewing that cigar, Michael sat slumped-back, pondering. His grandfather's face sure was straight out of 1920s Hollywood. He was as charismatic-looking as the great silent film star, Rudolph Valentino, Michael likened in his mind. Really, he was.

Michael later learned from a most surprising source that his grandfather was an ambitious man. He could have made it in Hollywood as easily as Valentino, Michael guessed. But Jimmy chose another road—one that put him in the wrong place at a wrong time and triggered ripples of strange karma to come.

At times, Michael thought dark angels had been hovering over his family. He imagined they had been conjuring debts to pay for sins of the father. The events that followed the shooting of Michael's grandfather made his worry unsurprising.

TWO

Taking It to the Grave

Mesmerized by the photograph, Michael hearkened back to all those whispers he had heard in his youth, about his family's past. But the murmurs certainly hadn't divulged much in the way of details. Older family members were tight-lipped. Either they couldn't say or wouldn't say. He was only told that his grandfather had been murdered, but no one would suggest how or why. Of course, the *Brooklyn Daily Flyer* article told Michael the answer to the *how*, but not the *why*. He wondered if he would ever know.

Back in the day, when Michael was a young investigative journalist, he had wanted to interview his Grandmother Camila (also called Millie) to learn more about the family's dark side. Millie had been Jimmy's wife, and she was the mother of his four children. Raising all the children alone without Jimmy was a testament to her strength. Even back then, Michael believed there was a story to be told, in a series of articles or in a book. But before he had a chance to speak with her, she underwent risky bypass heart surgery in the spring of 1979. Up until the surgery, she was still a frisky lady at seventy-six years old. She was given the option by her doctor to hopefully have successful surgery and continue her frisky ways. Or she could opt out of the surgery—and as an extension, any high-level activity, like lovemaking, she might wish to enjoy.

Michael had heard through the family grapevine, gnarled as it was, that his grandmother had said, "I would rather be dead than not go to bed."

Her quip was classic.

Millie didn't survive the surgery. And many of the family secrets died with her on that operating table. Michael's emotions had been mixed. Mourning his grandmother, he also had been disappointed, regretting his chance to find out some truths. After many years had passed since her death, most members of the family's older generation, including Michael's father, had also died, burying with all of them yet more possible revelations. Members of the family's Baby Boomer generation, to which Michael belonged, remained mostly in the dark.

Of course, Michael did learn some bits and pieces of the family legacy from his father. But, at the time, those nuggets seemed to lie somewhere between family folklore and absolute truth.

Sadly, on the very day Michael turned fifty-eight years old, he ran out of time with his father. Nicky had died. For every birthday that followed, Michael would recall painful details of that day. A familiar story, it was in early springtime, and it involved heart surgery. Even in 2009, because of Nicky's age at eight-one years old and his family medical history, the surgery was considered a risk. His father's legal guardian at the time, as Nicky was in the early stages of dementia, Michael signed the hospital forms to move ahead with the operation. At Nicky's bedside before the operation, the two men had played poker for nickels to pass the time and take their minds off the surgery. Nicky, who was an avid poker player, was now gambling with his life.

During the poker game, Michael realized this moment might be the last time he would speak with his father, if history repeated itself. So, he stopped the card game to ask: "Dad, what more can you tell me about our family's past?"

Nicky repeated the stories Michael had heard before, such as their favorite one about Frankie Fortunato, the Hollywood actor in the family. Maybe it was the dementia that made Nicky sound like a broken record, with the needle getting stuck in a groove. Nevertheless, Nicky, now lucid, then made a curious remark that chilled Michael.

"There's more about our family than you know. But there are reasons preventing me from saying anymore."

Those were Nicky's last words before he went into surgery. Later, Michael got the bad news from a doctor who had come to get him. Seated, he could tell just by looking up at the doctor's facial expression and body language, with his head cast down, that it wasn't going to be good.

"I'm sorry, your father didn't make it. He died on the operating table." Michael, containing his anger, immediately had thought, *Crazy karma, just like his mother*. The doctor then brought Michael into a claustrophobic room to identify his father's body; it was the first time he'd had to identify a dead person. The experience unnerved him then ... and his memory of it still did.

A few days later, the family attended the funeral of Nicky Cimino at a cemetery on Staten Island.

There he was buried with his wife, Dee, who uncannily was born on *December 1, 1928.*

Yes, the same month and day as the supposed murder of Jimmy Cimino, Michael's grandfather.

So, to Michael, it appeared his parents had been a star-crossed couple. Dee had given Nicky direction from when they were teenagers until she died of cancer, which had metastasized to her brain. Nicky was lost for eleven years before he passed and could rejoin his beloved. Perhaps now their souls would find peace together in eternity, Michael prayed.

The funeral closed with the customary throwing of roses on Nicky's grave. As family members dispersed, Michael mourned for the man who always had been there for him. While words of *love* rarely were said between them, except for the most special of times, father and son had always felt the *love*. The words were not always needed; it was understood.

Those feelings would not wither. But Michael knew Nicky's death had also cut a big cord to the family's past, as many of its older generation's secrets went to his grave, too.

THREE

Breakthrough

The mystery of Michael's family history mounted for eight more years, after his father's passing. That was when he'd discovered the *Brooklyn Daily Flyer* story, then, sometime later, the photograph of his grandfather, thanks to his oldest cousin, Carolina. She had secretly held the photograph since her mother—Nicky's younger sister—passed away in very early 2017. And Carolina's mother had received the photograph from Grandmother Millie just before she died on the operating table. The photograph, which had been quietly passed along through three generations, compelled Michael to further research his grandfather's early death and family's past beyond the *Brooklyn Daily Flyer* article. That story had cracked open a door. Now he was motivated to go through that open door to see what was on the other side, where the truth could be distinguished from family folklore. He hoped.

The natural evolution of his search led back to Carolina. Being Grandmother Millie's first and closest grandchild, Carolina knew some of her intimate memories. Michael had missed out on a deep conversation with his grandmother, but he would not make that mistake twice. He called his cousin.

"Carolina, it's Cousin Michael. I'm looking at that wedding photograph of our grandfather as we speak, and it's pushing me to find out more about him. Is there anything Grandma might have shared with you about him and his supposed murder?"

Thankfully, Carolina didn't hesitate with her reply. "I know our grandmother was moonstruck by our grandfather's striking looks. He was a dapper, and this was decades before 'Dapper Don' Gotti became a mob boss and media star. I heard that our grandfather liked wearing custom-made, tailored suits and stepping out at night. But the two argued that night our grandfather was gunned down because Grandma hadn't picked up his blue suit at the cleaners. So, he stormed out on her and his four children. He went off to the pool hall. That's all I know about that night."

At the time of his dubious murder, the children of Millie and Jimmy Cimino were a little more than a month old to four and a half years old. Michael's father, Nicky, was their second-born at age three. And there was Nicky's older brother, Joey, and two younger sisters: Concetta, Carolina's mother, and the infant baby, Margherita. It seemed that night at home was the last time Michael's grandmother and the children, who were old enough to be awake, saw Jimmy.

"Grandma told me she tolerated our grandfather's incorrigible ways," Carolina continued. "But she said he always came home before the early morning. When he didn't come home for the first time, Grandma got a bad feeling. Seems her worry was real, as she always sensed he was looking over his shoulder."

Then Michael asked, "Do you remember anything else that might be a clue to what was going on with our grandfather? Why the murder that we heard about growing up together?"

Her answer near blew Michael away.

"Well, our great-grandmother, Grandma's mother-in-law, made bootleg gin in a bathtub at her Coney Island home during Prohibition. And she carried a gun in her apron. Evidently, she knew how to fire it. There was frequent danger of rival bootleggers looking to muscle in on her."

Carolina's next comment really struck a chord: "Our great-grandmother recruited her three young sons, Grandpa and his equally wild brothers, to sell her bootleg gin on the streets of Brooklyn at neighborhood speakeasies. That shady business may have had something to do with Grandpa's shooting."

Well, well ... finally, some clue, maybe, Michael thought with a grin. Little did he know the much grander reason behind the attack on his grandfather. Still, he was elated to put some small piece of the puzzle together.

And Michael was soon getting closer to a larger piece, the identity of Jimmy's shooter. Left standing to pursue that shooter were Jimmy's younger brother, Francesco, known as Fran, and Leonardo, the oldest brother whom everyone called Leo. All three brothers were named after their ancestors in a specific order of respect, an Italian tradition from the old country. Like Michael's grandfather, Uncle Fran and Uncle Leo had the Cimino swagger. They were good-looking men, both of whom easily attracted the ladies. But they weren't as charismatic as Jimmy, whose wedding picture radiated a special aura with perfect facial features and a luminous presence. Temperament-wise, Michael learned both Uncle Fran and Uncle Leo were quiet men but could be just as explosive as his grandfather—the kind of explosive personality that Don Vito Corleone sometimes portrayed in *The Godfather*. But long before Don Vito, the Cimino brothers were the model for that type of behavior, an explosiveness that was unexpected, erupting just when all seemed calm.

The brothers' personalities had to have been passed down by their mother—one way or the other. Perhaps their behavior was just in the bloodline, genetic. But Michael believed his great-grandmother also encouraged a street culture that sociologically affected the brothers' actions and destiny.

While on Brooklyn's streets, selling his mother's bootleg gin, Jimmy met the merry, lovely Camila, a.k.a. Millie. Soon after, Millie introduced her younger, more reserved sister, the petite and pigtailed Isabella, to young Fran. Instantly attracted to the brothers, the sisters married the Cimino boys. Interestingly, both couples' children and grandchildren all closely resembled each other because two sisters had married two brothers. But the legacy of their marriages overall took lamented twists and turns.

Michael had joined Carolina for coffee at her home a few weeks after their last conversation, and he asked for more details about these two marriages. The tale was becoming more intriguing with every word he heard from his oldest cousin.

"I know this from Grandma," she said. "Marrying the Cimino brothers was exciting at first, even dangerous. The sisters seemed to just revel in the danger." Her hands went flying in the air as she spoke, and then she leaned forward slightly over the table, adding in a lower voice, "But the danger turned into a nightmare."

FOUR

Breaking the Code of Silence

Michael soon discovered a vital source who would become a fountain of information. But this source dripped out whatever he knew slowly, yet steadily. That was his nature.

In the spring of 2018, Michael attended a funeral of the last family member left standing from the older generation. The deceased was the second wife of his father's older brother, Joey, whose first wife died of brain cancer many years before the same disease killed Dee, Nicky's wife. The funeral had kicked in those bad memories and reminded Michael of the dark angels that may have been following his family. To him, the commonalities just seemed too uncanny to be a coincidence.

At the traditional family lunch after the burial, Michael was seated next to a man who was not family blood but distantly related through marriage. He was tall and tanned with a full head of white hair—and his brash personality fit his physical presence. Always showing up at family weddings and funerals, "Big" Marcio, as he endearingly was called by everyone, liked to gossip.

While Michael quietly confided with Cousin Carolina about the *Brooklyn Daily Flyer* story, this man, nevertheless, overheard them. Then, he boldly interrupted to leak what *he* knew.

"Don't be too shocked about that newspaper

story," he said, as Michael anxiously anticipated what he'd be saying next. "All three Cimino brothers were very connected. Your grandfather, in fact, was the driver for Brooklyn gangster Frankie Uale."

The cousins stared at each other with mouths agape and eyes wide. All Michael could think at first was: *get outta here*. Then he paused to soak in this man's revelations that helped to frame the big picture. Driving Uale around town affirmed for Michael that his grandfather was more than just small-time. And Uale's enemies most likely were Jimmy's enemies.

Having lived in Brooklyn all his life, Michael knew well the story of Uale, who Americanized his name's spelling as "Yale," after the University. As the number two man to Al Capone, before Capone left Brooklyn to run Chicago, Yale was the borough's biggest bootlegger at the beginning of Prohibition. He also controlled Brooklyn's ice delivery business by selling "protection" and building monopolies. But Yale eventually had a falling out with Capone. Ultimately, the Brooklyn bootlegger was killed by a shotgun and submachine gun blast to his head while in his car in Sunset Park, Brooklyn on July 1, 1928. Michael's Grandfather Jimmy luckily escaped that shooting. Subsequently, the NYPD investigated and tied Capone to Yale's killing. But nothing stuck.

The underlying message about these new revelations was: Big Marcio had revealed what older family members probably knew but kept quiet for decades under a code of silence. That was the Italian way. So, Jimmy's perceived murder really appeared to have been a downright execution. And Michael, who always had been a white-collar worker on the outside of "the life," suddenly knew he was just two generational steps from a family of crime.

Hearing the words from Big Marcio cemented the *Brooklyn Daily Flyer* story of a gangland murder. His words were resounding, further awakening the whispers Michael had heard for nearly six decades.

Still, Michael refrained from jumping too harshly into rumor. Were the statements of that man just bluster, as if to show off that he knew more than anyone else? Or were they completely true? Wherever the truth lay, his compelling comments pushed Michael to keep exploring—and with added fervor—the mystery behind his grandfather's assassination story.

FIVE

The Fortunatos

During an awkward phone conversation following the funeral lunch, a "Pandora's Box" of more secrets was about to open. But the lid of that box suddenly was shut tight, just like that.

While browsing the internet, Michael discovered contact information for a distant third cousin who shared the same great-grandparents with him. He thought, *Wow, another family member who might know something!* The family tree had many branches, though few people on this tree—extensive as it was—had information for him. He hoped this cousin would change that dynamic.

The man was Frank Fortunato III, a lawyer out on the West Coast—and son of famed Hollywood actor, Frankie Fortunato. He also had managed the latter stages of his father's career until the actor passed away in 2010.

Michael would eagerly reach out to Frank but first refreshed his knowledge of the actor's life.

Frankie began acting on Broadway in the late '40s and later performed in literally hundreds of television shows and in a fine run of hit movies. This man's career had spanned four decades, linking him with all the big stars throughout that time. Just name the A-lister, and Frankie had probably worked with him or her. Michael remembered him as the famous screen star that he was. In fact, when Michael was a young man, he once met the actor—through Uncle Fran.

But there was something even more compelling about Frankie Fortunato's rise to fame—a fascinating story of prison-time connections that Michael knew about from his father, Nicky. He wondered if the actor's son knew the story, too.

Not able to wait any longer, Michael placed the call to his distant cousin, Frank.

A receptionist at the attorney's office said she'd see if Mr. Fortunato was available. Michael nervously anticipated the conversation as he waited for the lawyer to pick up the phone. *Hoping* the attorney would pick up, he was feeling tentative because the two men had never physically met—or even talked on the telephone. The seconds ticked away into minutes, and Michael was about to hang up. But he didn't. Something inside of him—an intuition that something was coming—tamped down his typical impatience for answers. He would wait.

"Hello, Frank, this is Michael Cimino. I'm not sure if you know me. My father, Nicky, and your dad were first cousins. And my grandfather, Vincenzo James Cimino, was your Grandmother Maria Elena's younger brother." Michael's introduction was not very exciting, but he felt he had to first explain the family ties—or he'd lose the man.

Frank simply replied, "I know of your father and grandfather." That was all he said. And Michael realized that getting him to talk would be as tedious as pulling teeth.

Okay, he thought, staying patient. Some awkward silence ensued, after which the two kin strangers did some dancing. Michael groping for the right words; Frank feeling him out.

How to get this call really rolling …

Michael decided to break the ice by paying reverence to Frankie Fortunato the actor, his father.

"Say, Frank, you know my dad and I followed your father's work throughout his career," Michael said proudly. "I remember my dad bringing me to meet him at Uncle Fran's home in Brooklyn in 1971, the year Uncle Fran died. You remember Uncle Fran?"

Michael could practically feel the lawyer cringe.

Frank, curtly said, "I do."

Clearing his throat, Michael continued. "Yeah, he suffered with lung cancer for six years before dying. I remember he was a heavy smoker."

Silence.

Then, "Well, Uncle Fran…" Frank started, and Michael waited for him to finish his thought.

But Frank stopped short there, causing another awkward pause, as if he was censoring his thoughts on Uncle Fran. Michael knew Frank had a story to tell but was holding *something* back.

He pressed on. "Yeah, so, we all listened in awe to your father's Hollywood stories. I wish I could have known your dad even better, but that was the only time we met. Still, memories of him and his stardom live on with me." Too much praise? Too little? Michael hoped he was striking the right balance.

"Oh yeah? In what way?" Frank's change in tone revealed he had been moved by Michael's last statement. Or at the very least, he was interested in what Michael meant.

Michael breathed a sigh of relief away from the phone's receiver. Then, he continued, "I still watch him on television in TV shows and movies, and I have a recording of his best performances. One of my favorites on the recording is the role he played as a gypsy in the 'Gypsy' episode from *One Step Beyond*, that paranormal TV show that originally ran for three seasons from early 1959 to mid-1961. *The Twilight Zone*, which attracted a similar audience, became legendary. But *One Step Beyond*, in my opinion, was more frightening. Anyway, he led that great prison escape with his cellmate, played by a very young Robert Blake."

Frank chuckled. "I do remember that one."

"*Your* father sent the recording with a letter to *my* father before they both died," Michael said, feeling like he was finally engaging his cousin. "In the letter, he said he wanted his Hollywood legacy passed down to my dad's descendants. Hence, the recording. But you probably already know that."

Michael paused. No response. After just seconds, to avoid another long silence, the former reporter added, "Your dad wrote to my father, *I'm dying now, Nicky, but when it's over, let your children and their children know who I am and my work.* I've kept his legacy going with my two daughters. And still boast to people I meet about the many roles of Frankie Fortunato, the actor in our family."

Frank didn't say much, other than a couple of *uh-huhs*, one *yup*, and some grunts like he was shifting in his chair. Surely, Michael's words had evoked some emotion in Frank. Maybe he was just reticent.

But he'd also gone silent when Michael had mentioned Uncle Fran.

Michael now was ready to cut to the chase, the real motive for his call. No more tap dancing. *Just do it*, he thought. "I'm trying to find out about my family's past, and I'm hoping that you can help me, Frank."

He quickly remarked, "Well, I know a lot!"

Exactly what Michael had been hoping to hear. But would Frank share what he knew?

Turned out, the answer to that question was *no*. When Michael said, "Tell me more," Frank just backed off—a complete one-eighty—as if suddenly he was wary of Michael, of where the conversation would lead, of what was around the next corner.

Frank said, "Sorry, I've got a client meeting now, but text me." Then he rattled off his cell phone number and hung up, leaving Michael a little dazed.

Their dialogue was done. The conversation wasn't satisfying enough for Michael but, to an extent, telling. The attorney's comment about his knowledge of the family had tantalized the once reporter, leaving him wanting more.

What did Frank III know that Michael did not?

~ ~ ~

Michael texted Frank a few days later, but several weeks passed and the lawyer still had not replied. Given the lack of response, Michael felt certain Frank was having second thoughts about revealing details of their family's past. He would need to better bond with Frank, build a level of trust.

But how?

Through a genealogy search, he traced their family's ancestry yet again, checking and rechecking, going back to their great-grandparents. He found another wedding photograph. This photograph was of their Great-grandfather Giuseppe Cimino and Great-grandmother Concetta.

Michael thought that if he sent the photograph of their great-grandparents to Frank, the attorney might open up to him. So, Michael acted on that idea, hoping the photograph would be the glue to bond them.

That same night, Frank phoned his distant cousin. "Michael, this is Frank Fortunato. Thank you for sending the photograph of our great-grandparents. I never saw any picture of them. In a way, it's revealing. My father's sisters on the East Coast all had agreed: 'He looks so much like Nicky Cimino, especially as the two men have been growing older.' I think this photo, knowing they shared the same grandparents, explains that resemblance."

There, a little bond, Michael thought. Their bonding now gave Michael the opening he needed. He pivoted and wasted no time digging in to discover the family history. "Frank, I'm hoping you can tell me about our family's past. The last time we spoke you said you knew a lot."

This time Michael emphasized *our*, rather than *my*, to better connect with his cousin. After all, although Frank was a Fortunato, the Cimino blood also flowed through his veins.

SIX

Tale of a Parallel
Love Murder

Perhaps Michael's psychology to closely bond with Frank Fortunato had come to fruition. Following a long pause, the lawyer relented.

"Okay, I'll tell you what I know," he said. "After my father died in 2010, I cleaned out his office and found a screenplay that he wrote hidden in his desk. You may know he wrote as well as acted. His movie script, however, stayed in his desk for years and never was produced."

The attorney had piqued Michael's curiosity. "What's significant about the script?"

"When my dad was writing the screenplay, he told me that he was basing the narrative on a story his mother, Maria Elena, had told him. The prologue to his script, named *Gravesend's Revenge*, showed that it was modeled after the 1852 French stage play about the Corsican brothers."

While Michael wondered how Frankie's movie script may have mirrored the French stage play, he knew the story of the Corsican brothers. Being a journalist, Michael had become well-read. He understood that the play originated from the classic novella *The Corsican Brothers*, by French novelist Alexandre Dumas.

Michael reviewed the play's plotline in his mind.

It involved two brothers, Louis dei Franchi and Fabien dei Franchi, both of whom fell in love with Madame Emilie de L'Lesparre of Paris. The story told of Louis traveling to the City of Light to pursue his love while Fabien stepped back and conceded Madame Emilie to his brother. But Louis was faced with yet another love triangle involving the madame. And he was killed in a duel when Madame Emilie's other pursuer, Chateau-Renaud, puts a sword through his chest in a jealous rage.

Continuing to think the plotline through to its end, Michael recalled how Louis's brother, Fabien, subsequently hunted Chateau-Renaud and promised to avenge his brother. The final act ended with Fabien and Chateau-Renaud engaging in a sword fight. Chateau-Renaud is killed, and Louis is avenged as promised.

"So, how was your father's script modeled after the French stage play?" Michael asked Frank.

"In my father's script, he characterizes two fictional brothers, much like Louis and Fabien of the famous literary Corsican brothers. Similarly, these two brothers from Brooklyn, based on Vincenzo James and Uncle Fran, are in love with a beautiful, young woman from the old neighborhood in Gravesend. There they first met her during the late 1920s."

Listening intently, Michael continued scribbling notes for his research.

Frank further explained, "In my father's script, the older brother, Luigi, goes back to a poolroom in Gravesend. He's drawn to the beauty of Emilia, who is now married to the poolroom's owner. When Luigi meets the newly married couple, he's discouraged but knows his time with Emilia has passed. He must bow out and go back to his own family but not before shooting a game of pool. It was during this game that a rival gangster from Manhattan sought to seduce Emilia, when Luigi intervened and was quickly shot dead by this gangster holding a gun in each hand." Fortunato paused, likely for effect, then said, "Like Louis of the Corsican brothers and Luigi from *Gravesend's Revenge*, it's believed your grandfather met the same fate as these fictional characters for the same reason."

Before Michael could respond, Frank added almost apologetically, "You said you wanted to know about your family's past. Well, now you know a big part."

Michael leaned back in his chair and let out a long breath, suggesting he felt satisfied now with Frank. "That's okay. I already heard about my grandfather being murdered and that his shooter swiftly left the crime scene." Michael scratched the stubble under his chin, something he habitually did when feeling inquisitive. "So, what was the resolution to your father's script? Frank said, "The younger brother, Fabio, heard about how his older brother was murdered in a Gravesend poolroom during the night. After hearing the news, the next morning Fabio went after the gunman from Manhattan. Through connections on the street, he knew where to find him."

Anxiously wanting to know how the story ended, Michael asked, "Where was the gunman hiding out?"

Fortunato concluded, "The gunman from Manhattan was holed up in the old Half Moon Hotel in Coney Island on Riegelmann Boardwalk at West 29th

Street. So, Fabio tracked the two-gun gangster to his room. He knocked quietly on the door and, posing as the hotel manager, told the gunman he had a phone call in the lobby. The hunted man slowly opened the door, and the younger brother whispered his own last name. Then, he gutted the gunman with a straight-blade dagger from stomach to throat—avenging his brother."

Excited by the graphic ending, Michael burst out, "That's an amazing tale! Do you really believe this is the story of my grandfather and Uncle Fran?"

Frank was emphatic. "Oh, yes! I believe they're one and the same."

SEVEN

Hunting "Diamond Dick"

Frankie Fortunato's script, written as historical fiction, closely matched some of the family whispers Michael had heard. But he could never confirm the buzz passed down over the years. The whispers hinted that Uncle Fran did avenge Jimmy—he did what he had to do, in his mind. But Frankie Fortunato's screenplay couldn't be a true validation of what had happened, despite his son's self-assuredness. Perhaps the script was where truth and myth overlapped.

After speaking with Frank, Michael contacted Big Marcio, thinking he might have more to share. While the man wouldn't talk about what had motivated the presumed murder of Jimmy—or perhaps he just didn't know—he did say, "Your grandfather's mother, Concetta, confronted young Fran about avenging his brother. She leaned on Fran more than Leo and had confidence in him. As the matriarch, she demanded that Fran find Vincenzo James's shooter and get justice for the family. She also instructed, when he found the assassin, to say softly, 'My name is Cimino.' And she continued, 'Then kill him. How you do it is up to you. Just get it done!' She reminded Fran that the family had enough money to keep the cops quiet and for a lawyer, if needed."

The reality of hunting this man was easier said

than done. Continuing to research archived newspapers, Michael discovered a *New York Daily Press* article from September 1932—about ten months after his grandfather's reported murder.

The headline?

"Brothers Track Killer; Arrest Solves Murder."

Michael immediately delved into the article, then sat back and whistled—it was a long, low tone of disbelief. Imagine Bogie's iconic whistle just after Bacall baited him in the film version of Hemingway's *To Have and Have Not*.

Well, this is a shocker was Michael's first thought. His next thought was that the people most shocked likely would have been other Cimino family members around at the time.

The story reported that while cruising Brooklyn's streets in a car, Brother Leo came along for the hunt as backup. Also in the car were sidekicks Mary "May" West (not to be confused with the Broadway stage actress of that time and future Hollywood sexpot) and another young Gravesend hood who "had sworn to put" the hunted man "on the spot."

That night the Cimino brothers' blood vendetta led to a double arrest of those doing the *hunting* and the *hunted*, according to the story. The arrests allegedly solved the so-called slaying of Vincenzo James Cimino. While the brothers were hunting their man, they were intercepted by NYPD officers who, after being tipped off, were trailing them.

The article revealed that when the driver, Fran Cimino, showed his driver's license, one officer seemed to recognize the Cimino name. The officers then searched the vehicle, finding powerful weapons, including several sawed-off shotguns and a machine gun.

After the first arrest of the two brothers and their accomplices, a Detective O'Farrell heard about it back at the Coney Island precinct, according to the story. He put two and two together, as he clearly knew the Cimino name. He had investigated Vincenzo James Cimino's believed murder ten months earlier.

The *Daily Press* then reported the detective got the Ciminos to admit their mission: "We're hunting the man who gunned down our brother," Fran Cimino admitted to Detective O'Farrell. Uncle Fran also identified the whereabouts of the hunted man after further questioning. The brothers conceded they were informed of his location by other enemies of this targeted assassin.

That same night Riccardo "Dick" Di Marco of Manhattan, alias "Diamond Dick" (known for donning flashy diamond jewels) was found, charged, and arrested for allegedly murdering Vincenzo James Cimino.

Jail Time

Another news story in the *Brooklyn Daily Flyer*, published the next morning, reported results of the double arrests: While the Cimino brothers and their sidekicks were held in the Raymond Street jail in Brooklyn, Diamond Dick was locked up in a Queens cell, even though he'd been arrested in Kings County. His attorney argued he feared for his life if confined with the Cimino brothers.

Serious prison time for the brothers took two different turns, according to a Sing Sing prison record. Leo Cimino, who sacrificed himself by taking the rap for a felony charge of weapons possession, was sentenced three to six years at Sing Sing. He would be eligible for parole in May of 1935, when, soon after, the confluence of events would shake the Cimino family once again. Meanwhile, Uncle Fran and his two sidekicks in the car were all noted as accomplices to the crime and discharged.

However, Michael couldn't find out what happened to Diamond Dick. Follow-up newspaper stories featuring a murder trial didn't appear in any of the New York papers. He also scoured the internet for Department of Corrections prison records and searched for courtroom transcripts, but nothing came up. Strangely, Diamond Dick possibly had gone underground or left the country, vanished. Perhaps he, too, had been discharged of the arrest. In his case, there may have been a lack of evidence—no body or smoking guns found, and no witnesses. Or maybe he finally did end up underground … literally.

Five Years Later:1937

Turned out that Uncle Fran ultimately was punished big time for the crime of first-degree manslaughter in the spring of 1937.

Jumping ahead decades later to the late 1950s, older family members, including Michael's father, told the clan's younger generation about Uncle Fran's payback: "He had waited several years to avenge James's assassination." At that time and throughout the following years, nobody revealed whom Uncle Fran had hunted down—only that he'd eventually caught up with Jimmy's shooter and finished the job. The manslaughter conviction, rather than first-degree murder, appeared plausible to Michael, as it was considered a "crime of passion."

When Michael had first heard the story as a youngster, he'd thought to himself: *Uncle Fran neither forgave nor forgot.* Michael had held him up on a pedestal. He wasn't the only one. Most of the family's younger generation idolized him for getting justice in the eyes of everyone in the clan.

The older generation said, "Uncle Fran went away to college"—the elders' euphemism for being sent to prison—"for finally avenging his older brother." This was the family folklore that was passed down to the younger generation.

Now, the mystery was unraveling even more. Recalling this old folklore and learning the identity of Jimmy's shooter—the man known as Diamond Dick—together were exponentially telling. And the excitement for Michael was in the journey of getting closer to something extraordinary. But the mystery was far from being completely solved, and there was still more work to do.

EIGHT

How the Shit Hit the Fan
in Carroll Gardens

A new wrinkle now demythologized Uncle Fran when Michael discovered a *Brooklyn Times-Gazette* story published on October 2, 1936. After a one-year manhunt, twenty-eight-year-old Uncle Fran had been arrested for suspected murder in the fall of 1936. But this arrest was not about the avenged murder the family's Baby Boomer generation had known. This reported murder charge told the story of Uncle Fran killing twenty-one-year-old John DeVito at the Grand Street Tavern in East Williamsburg, Brooklyn.

The *Times-Gazette* printed a provocative headline about Uncle Fran's capture and arrest: "Cops Smash Down Door, Suspect Seized in Year-Old Killing." The story was further hyped with a deck: "Small Arsenal Found, Leads to Second Arrest."

The arrests, as described in the story, appeared dramatic. After knocking and getting no response, NYPD cops crashed the door of an apartment on Carroll Street in Brooklyn's Carroll Gardens and seized Uncle Fran.

Detectives at the scene said they also found a lady friend with him. Sleeping in separate beds, it seemed there wasn't anything sexual between them. Their meeting, as it was later inferred, appeared to be strictly business. According to the story, a small arsenal of weapons and ammunition was found in the apartment, too. The weapons included two rifles, two 38-caliber automatics and a straight-blade dagger, along with 500 rounds of ammunition.

After seizing all weapons and ammunition, Detective Henson, who was at the scene of the arrest, said, "Let's get Cimino's brother, Leo, in for questioning."

Uncle Leo was well known around the NYPD; at that time, he had thirteen prior arrests from robbery to assault. By the time he died, he'd been arrested seventeen times. While growing up, Michael believed Uncle Leo lived in the shadow of his brothers. Vincenzo James had drawn public attention from the horrific news of his reported murder. And Uncle Fran had become adored by younger family members since being perceived as his brother's avenger. But Uncle Leo was no wallflower. He was a ruthless badass with a drug addiction. Nevertheless, there was no evidence linking him to the murder of John DeVito. Recently paroled from Sing Sing in the spring of 1935, he was dismissed of any charges.

According to the reporting, the same detective had asked, "Who has legal residence to this place?" And Fran Cimino had shot back, "This my place."

The mystery woman with Uncle Fran claimed she was just an acquaintance of his and had not seen him in two years, based on the story. "After he called me," she said, "I came to see him. We stayed up late talking and later fell asleep." Then the woman added, "The firearms and ammunition belong to my brother, but Fran Cimino owns the dagger."

The story also revealed that the woman's brother was soon picked up and arrested on a Sullivan Law charge. The New York State law, which took effect in 1911, required a license for possessing a firearm small enough to be concealed. When questioned by the police, the woman's brother, a known gunrunner among gangsters, said he'd smuggled the small arsenal into the country from Nicaragua.

The story didn't disclose any reason the arsenal had landed in the Carrol Street apartment. Uncle Fran, however, was the target of a police manhunt, indicted for murdering young DeVito at the Grand Street Tavern. So, for Michael, it didn't seem unusual that his uncle would want some firepower for protection—and the woman had weaponized him, fulfilling just that need.

The article summarized that Fran Cimino had confronted DeVito at the Grand Street Tavern on July 12, 1935—and they argued. Suddenly, several shots were fired, killing DeVito. Police found the smoking gun in a trash can on Humboldt Street, just around the corner from Grand. The clincher: a female eyewitness identified Fran Cimino as the trigger man. An indictment followed.

At first glance, it appeared the family folktale of Uncle Fran avenging his brother Jimmy had covered up the true crime. An *aha* moment for Michael, the myth had now looked dispelled. This was the myth seemingly spun by older family members so that Uncle Fran would be remembered as a sympathetic hero to the younger generation and future descendants.

But after thinking twice, Michael believed Uncle Fran might have also sliced up two-gun Diamond

Dick with a dagger somewhere in time. He recalled that a straight-blade dagger had been found in Uncle Fran's Carrol Street place, possibly the same dagger depicted in Frankie Fortunato's movie script. And Michael couldn't find any record of Diamond Dick after 1932—the year of the double arrest. Like Grandfather Jimmy had disappeared, based on all Michael had learned, Diamond Dick may have evaporated into thin air, too. One bad turn deserved another—a perfect revenge murder!

NINE

*Two-Headed Lady Fingers
a Trigger Man*

In April of 1937, Uncle Fran, now twenty-nine years old, was on trial for murder in the first degree. After the one-year manhunt and his capture for the charge of killing young John DeVito, Uncle Fran was facing a jury in front of unsympathetic Judge Peter B. Bragante. A guilty verdict for first-degree murder, at this time in New York State, meant life in prison or, worse yet, the death penalty.

Michael sat at his desk with the courtroom transcripts. For comfort, he had a hot cup of coffee in hand and a Cuban cigar, kept moist and fresh in his humidor, ready to be lit. He took a careful sip and lit up, then reviewed the courtroom drama for the fourth time—it was that engrossing to him. Not so much for the play-by-play of the crime itself, but because of what ultimately had happened during the trial.

On the first day in the courtroom, the defense pleaded not guilty, and opening arguments were given by both sides. The statements were equally short in length, which Michael guessed was pleasing to the jury—to have avoided the typically long-winded explanations of the legal community.

The prosecution simply stated they had evidence and a key witness.

The defense said Uncle Fran was provoked, and therefore, the shooting was not premeditated.

Next up was the prosecution and its first witness, a man named Mickey Collins, who had been the bartender at the Grand Street Tavern on the night of the shooting. Collins confirmed the two men, Fran and John, had been seated together and drinking at the bar. He couldn't remember exactly how many drinks they'd had—just that it was more than a few, enough to cause some agitation.

PROSECUTOR: *Mr. Collins, did you observe the defendant getting angry at any time during his encounter at the bar with the deceased, John De-Vito?*

WITNESS: *Let's just say he didn't seem happy over some arguing with the deceased.*

The prosecution abruptly ended the questioning and stepped away. Now it was the defense team's turn to question the bartender.

While depicting the deceased as hotheaded and drunk, the prosecution objected to some leading questions directed at the witness. Overall, the defense delivered an acceptable query.

DEFENSE: *What did the deceased argue about with the defendant during the night in question?*

WITNESS: *They argued over splitting up money from hijacking a truck full of silks.*

DEFENSE: *What did you specifically hear from the argument?*

WITNESS: *The deceased was angry that part of the split was given to the defendant's brother, Leo Cimino, who was high on narcotics during the hijacking. He didn't think the defendant's brother deserved a share of the money because his recklessness put everyone else from the crew in danger.*

DEFENSE: *Was the defendant's brother nearby at the time of the argument?*

WITNESS: *Yes, Leo Cimino was there, but not at the bar. He was sitting at a table with some other fellas. They'd all come in together, Fran Cimino included.*

DEFENSE: *So, you can see that the defendant would be especially sensitive about an insult directed at his brother. Agreed?*

PROSECUTION: *Objection, Your Honor. Leading the witness.*

JUDGE: *Objection is sustained. The jury will disregard the question referring to the defense's statement, and the witness will not answer.*

DEFENSE: *I'll rephrase my question. What was the defendant's reaction when the deceased insulted Leo Cimino?*

WITNESS: *The defendant got visibly upset, and one word led to another between the defendant and the deceased.*

DEFENSE: *How did the argument end?*

WITNESS: *When the defendant said his brother 'was at risk as much as everyone else in the crew,' the deceased laughed in his face. The argument reached a boiling point. Then the defendant got explosive and impulsively reached for his gun.*

DEFENSE: *Did the defendant's action appear irresistible?*

WITNESS: *Yes.*

DEFENSE: *As a result of the defendant's irresistible impulse, which does not suggest premeditation, what happened next?*

WITNESS: *I believe that I heard gunshots coming from different directions. That's all I know.*

And that was the end of the first day of Uncle Fran's trial. On the second day, the prosecution called their next witness, Detective McMann with the Brooklyn division of the NYPD.

PROSECUTION: *Detective McMann, how did you first get involved with the murder of John DeVito?*

WITNESS: *I was assigned to the Grand Street Tavern crime scene where DeVito was killed the night of July 12, 1935.*

PROSECUTION: *What did you see when you arrived there?*

WITNESS: *DeVito was dead on the floor, close to the door. He was shot several times.*

PROSECUTION: (Facing the jury) *I hold up Exhibit A, the gun that killed Mr. DeVito. Detective, can you tell us what kind of gun this is?*

WITNESS: *Yes, it's a 38-caliber automatic with a pearl handle.*

PROSECUTION: *Did the detective squad assigned to the crime scene find this weapon?*

WITNESS: *Yes, we found it in a trash can on Humboldt Street, around the corner from Grand.*

PROSECUTION: *How did you connect the defendant to this weapon?*

WITNESS: *We connected him to the weapon in two ways. First, after questioning several people who were at the tavern that night, one woman, AnnMarie Morano, came forward and said she witnessed the killing. Miss Morano said she saw Fran Cimino pull*

*the trigger of that gun. She recognized the pearl han-
dle and identified the defendant from his mugshot.
Secondly, this gun comes from Nicaragua. When we
arrested Fran Cimino at his Carrol Street apartment
after a one-year manhunt, we found multiple weapons, including two other 38-caliber automatics,
which we learned had come from Nicaragua.*

The prosecution stepped down, and the defense chose not to cross-examine.

Day Three was livelier, with the prosecution call-ing AnnMarie Morano to the witness stand.

PROSECUTOR: *Miss Morano, where were you the night John DeVito was killed at the Grand Street Tavern?*

WITNESS: *I was sitting at a table in the tavern with my companion. We were waiting to order drinks.*

PROSECUTOR: *So, did you order?*

WITNESS: *No, we never got the chance.*

PROSECUTOR: *Then can we establish that you and your companion were clearheaded that night and aware of what was happening around you?*

WITNESS: *Yes.*

PROSECUTOR: *I understand that you once worked at the tavern. What was your job?*

WITNESS: *I was a hat-check girl.*

PROSECUTOR: *Was the defendant, Fran Ci-mino, a regular customer at the tavern?*

WITNESS: *Yes.*

PROSECUTOR: *So, can we conclude that you know the defendant's face very well and would not mistake his identity?*

WITNESS: *That's right.*

PROSECUTOR: *Were you seated at a table close to the bar where the argument between the deceased and defendant occurred?*

WITNESS: *Yes.*

PROSECUTOR: *What did you hear during the argument?*

WITNESS: *I overheard the words "silks" and "money" several times.*

PROSECUTION: *How did the argument end?*

WITNESS: *John DeVito got up and started to leave the tavern. When he reached the door, the defendant fired four shots at him.*

The prosecution concluded their questioning, turning it over to the defense attorney, who indeed wanted to cross-examine Miss Morano.

DEFENSE: *I want to remind you, Miss Morano, that you took an oath to tell the truth. I understand that you now have a job in Coney Island. Please tell the court your profession.*

WITNESS: *I'm an entertainer.*

DEFENSE: *What kind of an entertainer? Are you a singer or dancer?*

WITNESS: *No, I'm an illusionist.*

DEFENSE: *Where do you perform this illusion?*

WITNESS: *At the* (witness puts her head down and pauses for a short time) *Coney Island freak show* (people of the court laugh).

PROSECUTOR: *Objection, Your Honor. Defense is trying to discredit the witness.*

JUDGE: *Objection is not sustained. Defense has the right to establish the witness's line of work, no matter the kind of work. Defense may continue questioning the witness.*

DEFENSE: *Thank you, Your Honor. Miss Morano, what illusion do you perform at the freak show?*

WITNESS: *I'm the two* (short pause) *two-headed woman* (people of the court gasp and laugh).

DEFENSE: *Well, I suppose two heads are better than one* (people of the court laugh). *So, how do you perform this illusion? Certainly, you have only one real head* (people of the court laugh).

WITNESS: *A plaster cast of my head, with my face painted on it by an artist, is attached to my left shoulder. Then, a wig that matches my hair style and color is added to the cast.*

DEFENSE: *That is an ingenious illusion. I bet that trick really pulls the wool over your audience's eyes, right?*

PROSECUTION: *Objection, Your Honor. Defense is leading the witness.*

JUDGE: *Objection is sustained. The jury will disregard the question, and the witness will not answer it. Defense may continue questioning the witness.*

DEFENSE: *Let me put it another way, then. When you perform your two-headed woman act, do members of the audience believe you have two heads because their eyes may be playing tricks on them?*

WITNESS: *Well,* (short pause) *yes.*

DEFENSE: *And that is the point! The tavern's bartender, Mr. Collins, testified that gunshots came from different directions. So, did your eyes and ears possibly play tricks on you, making it difficult to pinpoint the shooter who had fired the deadly shot?*

WITNESS: *I believe the defendant pulled the*

trigger and shot John DeVito.

DEFENSE: *Your statement does not sound as emphatic now.*

As the prosecution objected to the defense's last comment, the defense attorney finished with "I rest my case."

Michael wondered why the defense used this "tricks of the eye" angle with AnnMarie Morano. Originally, the defense had been focused on the idea that Uncle Fran had indeed shot DeVito, but it was provoked and *not* premeditated. So, it was *not* first-degree murder. Now it seemed the defense was suggesting that perhaps their client had not shot DeVito at all. Michael, at first, couldn't comprehend the defense attorney flipping his strategy. Then, after mulling it over, he determined this lawyer hadn't been so sure he'd win with the "provocation" strategy. Michael believed the attorney had adjusted on the fly, seizing the chance to discredit AnnMarie Morano's testimony and raise some shadow of doubt with the jury. Judge Bragante had reminded the jury, even before witnesses had been called to testify, about shadow of doubt and how it requires a not-guilty verdict. Michael figured the jury members had that idea well ingrained in their minds when they decided their verdict.

After AnnMarie Morano's testimony, a second witness named Charles Ricco, who was Morano's companion during the night of the shooting, also testified against Uncle Fran. He, too, spoke about an argument between Uncle Fran and the deceased over the spoils of a silk-truck hijacking. Ricco identified Uncle Fran as the shooter who killed John DeVito.

Ricco's credibility, however, appeared question-able. Reportedly, he was brought down to testify from Woodbourne Prison in New York State, where the man was serving time for robbery. His prison background was noted in the *Daily Press* story of April 21, 1937, with the incredible headline: "Woman Freak Testifies She Saw Slaying."

No doubt, both key witnesses had questionable credibility. And the evidence was not strong enough for the jury to find Uncle Fran guilty of murder in the first degree. But the jury did find him guilty of first-degree manslaughter on April 23, 1937. The conviction was defined as a killing committed in the "heat of passion" that results from provocation. Evidently, the jury believed John DeVito had caused Uncle Fran to act irrationally; the defense's primary argument won over the jury after all.

But was it really a win? The answer had Michael shaking his head after Judge Bragante delivered his sentence.

The Sentencing

On May 10, 1937, Uncle Fran was sentenced to a maximum of thirty years at Sing Sing for killing John DeVito. The long-term sentence was warranted in Judge Bragante's mind because of Uncle Fran's prior robbery conviction. Michael pictured Uncle Fran standing before the judge and thinking that his past life in the fast lane had finally caught up with his future. Then, Michael imagined his uncle visualizing the prison bars and dwelling about all that *time* ahead of him. His future looked so bleak.

But Judge Bragante thought Uncle Fran had actually "got a break" when the jury found him guilty of manslaughter in the first degree, according to the next day's story in the *Daily Press*. The judge's view was reflected in the story's headline: "'You're Lucky,' Judge Tells Jailed Killer."

According to the story, Judge Bragante opined outspokenly, "If another jury had reviewed this case, Fran Cimino would be found guilty of murder, first degree. In my opinion, that was the crime he committed."

Uncle Fran's attorney had moved to set aside the verdict altogether. He believed the jury wasn't justified in returning a manslaughter verdict when the State had charged Uncle Fran with murder in the first degree. But Judge Bragante denied the request.

Reportedly, the judge had said, "If you'd made that motion on the day this defendant was convicted, I would have granted it, but the People now have lost control of their witnesses."

Judge Bragante never softened. He was of Italian descent and likely wanted to separate himself from the criminals of his own kind. So, the judge was especially tough on them in public. But to be fair, Judge Bragante had been even-handed during the trial.

Uncle Fran was now off to prison, far from the familiar streets of Brooklyn. He would have to adjust to prison culture—long term. No option.

TEN

Dannemora:
The Church of St. Dismas Rises

Although Uncle Fran initially was sentenced to a maximum of thirty years at Sing Sing by Judge Bragante, his time there didn't last long. In the late 1930s, he was moved from the prison, which ominously still stands with its inmates overlooking the Hudson River in Ossining, New York (hence, the origin of the prison slang "up the river") to the Clinton Correctional Facility.

Michael knew of the Clinton penitentiary. But he decided to upgrade his knowledge of it with additional research, especially since his own flesh and blood had once resided there. He refreshed his memory on the facility's history, and in doing so, learned some interesting facts—or at least possibilities of truths—about his family history.

Commonly called "Dannemora," the prison was built in the village of Dannemora, near Dannemora Mountain, in Auburn, New York. The mountain is part of the vast Adirondack Mountains, ascending just twelve miles from the facility and teasingly visible from the yard. A convict could easily dream of escaping and getting lost in those mountains forever. But far away in the North Country of upstate New York, the reality of Dannemora is bitterly referred to as "Little Siberia" by its convicts because it is so cold and remote. It is just twenty-five miles from the Canadian border and fifteen miles east to Lake Champlain, where   ferryboats ride to the border of Vermont.

Built in 1844, Dannemora has been known for confining the most dangerous criminals in New York State. The penitentiary continued the culture of the Auburn System for prisons, established in 1818. The system, which was considered less costly, once kept prisoners in solitary and total silence and constrained them to prison labor.

On July 22, 1929, the largest riot in prison history erupted at Dannemora. The uprising involved 1,300 prisoners trying to escape by attacking its walls and setting buildings ablaze. During the riot, three guards were killed while others were beaten.

Eventually, the prisoners backed down, but the riot resulted in prison reform. Following these reforms, Uncle Fran and a slew of infamous convicts were confined behind the walls of Dannemora. Notorious criminals such as crime boss Charlie "Lucky" Luciano, serial rapist and murderer Joel Rifkin, rapper Tupac Shakur, preppy murderer Robert Chambers and killers and escapees Richard Matt and David Sweat benefited from these reforms at different times throughout history. Still, they all were believed to be under the maximum grip of this prison until Matt and Sweat shockingly escaped in 2015. Although the system had let its guard down allowing the escape, this place has continued to be no pen for white-collar crime. Dannemora, with its once dungeon as solitary, has always been a hellhole for serious hard time. Only one heavenly haven would appear like an oasis in its hellish environment.

Ultimately, Uncle Fran served only sixteen years of his sentence, but it was still a long stretch. His sentence, after legal review, was shortened because of a technicality involving Judge Bragante's decision. Through an unusual twist of fate, Uncle Fran was freed from Dannemora in 1953 and reunited with his wife, Isabella, and the rest of his family.

Michael's earliest memory of meeting Uncle Fran was when he was eight years old. The year was 1959. His father took him to visit Uncle Fran and Aunt Isabella at their home on 19th Avenue in Bath Beach, Brooklyn. Their two children, James (known as Jamesy by everyone in the family) and Connie, were grown and gone from the home at that time.

First impressions of Uncle Fran stuck with Michael. And these impressions vividly materialized whenever he visited the Staten Island cemetery, where Uncle Fran, Aunt Isabella, and Michael's mom and dad were buried. Moreover, all the researching into his family tree caused these memories to flourish again.

Michael remembered Uncle Fran was tall and lean with olive skin and dark, brown eyes. He reminded Michael of the great dancer and triple-threat performer Fred Astaire, only with a darker complexion. Coincidentally, Uncle Fran was known to be a ballroom dancer like Astaire. He also played the mandolin and sang like Astaire, as both men were multitalented.

But most memorable of all were Uncle Fran's oil paintings that decorated the walls of his home. Michael knew that Uncle Fran had learned to paint at

Dannemora. He was the prison's self-taught van Gogh. His paintings, which illustrated the isolation and loneliness at Dannemora, were brilliant works, in Michael's opinion.

Michael would give anything to have just one of these paintings in his possession. But nobody alive in the Cimino family knew what had happened to those pictures that hung in the rooms of his uncle's home—they were a lost treasure. Another family mystery.

Michael did know, from his father Nicky, that those paintings had attracted a priest at the prison. He was Father Ambrose Hyland of the Church of St. Dismas, the Good Thief. The church, which commemorates one of the criminals who was crucified next to Jesus and forgiven by Christ, was the first in the country to be built behind prison walls. Nicky had often spoken of Father Hyland, whose dream was to build the Church of St. Dismas. The Father's dream came true. The church was built—all of stone—by Dannemora's inmates sometime between 1939 and 1941. These stones were salvaged from the site's existing structures, such as the first cell block that had no longer confined convicts. Dedicated on August 28, 1941, this new house of the holy became a solace to the inmates and historical landmark.

Michael learned the reason Uncle Fran was relocated to Little Siberia from his dad. It was because he was skilled at cutting and setting stone and marble. Tradesmen like him were needed to build the church. All three Cimino brothers, in fact, had learned the trade from their father (Michael's great-grandfather) who knew this work from Naples, Italy.

Bringing his trade, Giuseppe Cimino came to America with his children—Vincenzo James, Leonardo, and Maria Elena—and his wife Concetta on the ship called *S.S. Madonna* on September 11, 1907.

Michael knew about the family's emigration by discovering the ship's manifest. And he understood that Uncle Fran and a younger sister, Dorinda, were born later in America.

Despite their criminal history, Michael's father Nicky reminded him, pridefully, how the Ciminos also made their mark helping to build many of the great, old, marble-filled movie theaters in New York City. So if not for learning to cut and set stone and marble, Uncle Fran conceivably never would have met Father Hyland.

Life was certainly a series of interlocking events, making the meeting between convict and priest another link in the family's long and twisted chain.

Many years before Nicky died, Michael asked his dad, "How did the relationship between Uncle Fran and Father Hyland begin and then grow?"

Nicky noted, "Father Hyland loved art and was sympathetic to the prisoners, like Jesus was to St. Dismas. Father was the original *hoodlum* priest. So, their friendship was destined."

God, Dignity and Redemption

Interestingly, Father Hyland also had Hollywood connections. Michael first learned about these connections from his dad, but an obscure story that he found on the internet confirmed his dad's tale. As the internet story goes, a group of Hollywood executives (from MGM) met the priest to discuss making a movie about building the Church of St. Dismas. That meeting was held in 1946. Out in Hollywood, the Father told the moviemakers that they should convey his mission on film: *To help the prisoners find hope and feel a sense of belonging to something greater than themselves, even though they had been locked away from society.* The Father believed that men in prison could change and lead a useful life through their own dignity, given to them by God. The movie was never made because negotiations broke down due to differing visions for the film; Hollywood, typically, imagined more violence and less redemption. But Father Hyland's connections with these Hollywood heavyweights remained with him.

Written by Patrick T. Reardon, this internet story focused on the writer's remembrances of a little-known novel that he read as a twelve-year-old in 1962. It was just before he was planning to enter a high school seminary and the start of the Second Vatican Council. Entitled *Gates of Dannemora*, the 1951 novel told the story of Father Hyland and his church. Cast away by Catholic hierarchy because of his rebellious ways, the "Robin Hood" priest and his merry men of Dannemora built the Church of St. Dismas, despite political and financial hurdles. Although historical, the book reads like a novel because the stone builders' identities had been disguised by the author due to their deeply personal, criminal records.

In the internet story, the boy-turned-man, who had read the novel many years earlier at an impressionable age, always remembered this description of the priest: He was an imposing figure at six-foot two-inches tall. The Father who got in trouble with church authorities for being "too hip" was imprinted in his memory. The man never forgot the priest who had been reassigned to Dannemora and made religious converts of dangerous criminals. That's how, years later, Michael rediscovered this story about Father Hyland luring Hollywood. The discovery supported Michael's recollection of the priest and producers, as told by his dad, Nicky.

"After Uncle Fran and Father Hyland grew closer, the Father made a proposal to him," Nicky had said many times to Michael over the years. "The Father offered to help anyone in our family who wanted to go to Hollywood to become an actor through his connections."

Michael immediately had been captivated by Nicky's Hollywood story. And the tale only got better.

"So, what happened next?" Michael had asked his dad, anxiously wanting to learn who was the chosen one.

"My Cousin Frankie Fortunato, who was pursuing an acting career after coming home from fighting in the Philippines during World War II, got his big break. Frankie just finished a role on Broadway in 1949, when Father Hyland took him under his wing and brought him out to Hollywood. The Father was a celebrity in his own right. Because of the church's historic status and the priest's unusual flock of inmates, he also had a following outside Dannemora. Father Hyland then introduced Frankie to some of the most influential directors and producers of that time. And Frankie's Hollywood career began to take off."

What a saga, thought Michael. To him, Nicky's story seemed even more incredible all these years later than when he first heard it. Hearing the story when younger, Michael had been more gullible. He ate up all those stories and easily believed them. But Reardon's preteen impression of the Father and *Gates of Dannemora,* which backed up Nicky's story, made the tale seem even more amazing and authentic.

ELEVEN

"Greeney" and Uncle Fran

Michael knew he now had to read the book for himself. He wanted to know from the very pages about the priest, about whether Uncle Fran might be a character in this novel. And, if so, what more could he learn about Uncle Fran from the book—and maybe even some new clue about the Cimino family's secret past.

Michael searched for the book on Amazon, luckily locating one remaining rare, first edition. Priced at just thirty dollars, he quickly ordered the vintage book. No hesitation, as he didn't want anyone else to snap it up. He waited anxiously to receive it in the mail, and when it arrived, he literally ripped the packaging away so that he could finally hold the treasure in his hands. If Michael knew of the book's delicate condition, he might have been more careful. The book's binding was frayed; the cover stained, and the pages were yellowish-brown and dry from oxidation. Though worn, it was the content of the story that mattered most.

The Foreword quoted Father Hyland, who inspired the novel: "This book presents a true story of a group of individuals about whom you probably know very little. Yet you and I might easily have become part of this group. The gulf which separates us and them is not nearly so impassable as some of us like to suppose." The Father's point was that the prisoners of Dannemora embodied the human spirit as much as anyone on the outside. The convicted were alive—and human beings. Everybody was looking for love and redemption. Only the prison walls separate those on the inside from those on the outside.

After reading about a third of the book, Michael remained focused on Father Hyland's fortitude to fulfill his dream of building the church. But Michael's main mission was to identify Uncle Fran as a character. He came across a section of the book that portrayed a prisoner named "Greeney," who closely resembled Uncle Fran's demeanor and situation. Although the inmates' real names had been disguised, Michael felt in his gut Greeney was Uncle Fran.

Reading about Greeney being visited by his wife, Michael visualized it was Uncle Fran meeting Aunt Isabella behind the walls. Strangely, the wife in the book was named "Millie," the name of Isabella's sister. Perhaps the author's intention was to cloak Isabella while hinting about her real identity. Describing the husband-and-wife meeting in straight narrative, Michael read between the lines and imagined, with his ideas running wild, a conversation that may have happened between his aunt and uncle.

"I'm smiling to see you and the baby," Michael fantasized Uncle Fran saying to his wife on the other side of the plate-glass window.

As told in the book, it was the first time Greeney had seen his new baby. This development was close to the events in Uncle Fran's and Aunt Isabella's life. Michael had heard through family whispers about a second boy born to his aunt and uncle. The child, evidently conceived before Uncle Fran was sent to prison, sadly had died very young.

Michael continued to let his imagination run …

"I would have come sooner, but I was so angry with you for leaving me alone," Aunt Isabella said. "But after I had the baby, I felt different. Women feel different about their man after having a baby."

"I'm ashamed, even though I feel like I'm innocent," lamented Uncle Fran. "And I worry about our marriage and the children."

Michael envisioned that Uncle Fran, trying to speak with a window between his wife and him, would have been reminded of the great divide separating them. He was on the inside looking out.

But the prisoners were not supposed to show fear, according to the book's narrative. That was part of the prison code. Instead, there were just wise cracks about the wife and window to mask any worry. Michael thought, *You don't wear emotion on your sleeve; don't want to bring down the other men. Otherwise, they will weaken and crack, maybe.*

Visiting time was up, as the book noted that Greeney walked away stoic. But the man knew, as described in the narrative, he'd rather not see anyone from the outside. Mentally, it seemed healthier to stay within the walls and not be reminded of the outside world. On the inside, all the inmates thought alike—it felt safe.

Then, as Michael read in the book, another visitor showed up for Greeney. This time the visitor was his brother. Michael, once again, let his thoughts get carried away. He imagined that brother might have been

Uncle Leo. The book talked about this brother getting the "brush-off" from Greeney. Michael understood that if the brother was, in fact, Uncle Leo, then getting the brush-off made sense. *There probably was some tension between the brothers after all that had happened,* thought Michael. *Maybe even the wrong brother had been convicted,* he guessed.

But the conversation, before this brush-off, boiled down to a single tattle. The brother in the book said, "Millie's running around. She had the baby and was talking divorce." Michael, even if he had imagined wildly what Uncle Leo might have said, could not have dramatized it better. While the marriage now seemed on thin ice, Michael believed Greeney (or Uncle Fran, in his mind) perhaps felt relieved. No longer was there any pressure of his obligation to their marriage, with him on the inside and her miles and miles away on the outside. Getting together again appeared unlikely anyway to the man behind the walls, based on the novel. Too much separating them: the walls, time, and a lot of baggage.

Sometimes, however, making plans can result in the unexpected. Michael knew Uncle Fran eventually had experienced a big surprise. Meeting his aunt and uncle in the late 1950s, when they were back together, proved the unexpected had happened. For Michael, how that all had developed was yet to be learned.

TWELVE

Finding the "Holy Grail"

After being engulfed by *Gates of Dannemora*, Michael felt he had to share the contents with the one family member who would most identify with the story. He was the only living grandson of Uncle Fran. And by reaching out to him, Michael would truly uncover the secrets to Uncle Fran's inside story—life behind the walls of Dannemora—in his uncle's words. This new discovery went beyond Michael merely imagining the Greeney character as Uncle Fran.

The secrets were literally in the hands of Uncle Fran's grandson, James Cimino Jr. Named after his father, Jamesy, the first namesake of the vanished Vincenzo James, Michael hadn't seen his cousin since they were children and both naïve to their family's history. He found James Jr. on Facebook and called him over fifty-five years later. Their reintroduction to each other was warm and friendly, and the conversation flowed, as if hardly any time was lost between them. The experience was so unlike Michael's awkward initial talk with his distant cousin in California, Frank Fortunato.

This conversation between Michael and James Jr. lasted three hours—they both had much catching up to do about the Cimino family background. And having the same last name helped connect them.

Michael first told James that he was researching the secrets of the Cimino family and stumbled across some interesting discoveries. He explained that doing the research came natural to him, as he used to be an investigative journalist. At the onset, Michael didn't want to say too much about what he knew. He worried that James might be sensitive to the dark history and didn't want to disrespect how his cousin's mother and father may have treated the truth. Michael believed he first had to find out what James Jr. already knew to ease into the conversation.

"Do you know anything about your grandfather's past, James?"

Bluntly, he said, "I know my grandfather was sentenced to prison for first-degree manslaughter when he was twenty-nine years old. Then he was released after spending sixteen years behind bars."

Michael realized James's reply was the opening he needed to introduce him to the novel about Father Hyland. "You know, James, I just read a book called *Gates of Dannemora*, which tells the story of this prison and building the landmark Church of St. Dismas on the inside. You probably know this is where your grandfather did most of his time. While the book focuses on Father Ambrose Hyland, who led the building of this church, it also profiles the inmates who helped build it of stone. The prisoners' names are fictional to protect them, but I believe I've identified your grandfather in this book. So, he'll always live on in this way. What do you think about that?"

James replied, "I'd like to see for myself. My grandfather and I grew close, so I got to know him. I'm sure I'd be able to recognize him in this book.

And I'll tell you another story that really immortalizes my grandfather. When I was younger, I operated an auto body shop on Staten Island, where a man came in and talked about my grandfather being memorialized in an unusual way. When he saw the Cimino name on my business card, he asked: 'Are you related to Fran Cimino?' I told him my older brother was Fran, but he and his young son were killed in a car accident coming home from a skiing trip. Then, the man explained, 'Your brother would have been too young to be this person I have in mind.'"

Michael knew this man must have been thinking about Uncle Fran.

James then put the story to rest: "I told him my grandfather was Fran Cimino. The guy says, 'When I was away at Dannemora prison, every day I passed a plaque on the Church of St. Dismas with Fran Cimino's name engraved on it.' I told him that person definitely was my grandfather, that he was imprisoned at Dannemora and helped build the church. I knew about the Church of St. Dismas long before speaking to this man, Michael. But I didn't know about the plaque. So, I was proud to have learned my grandfather would be forever connected to that church. I'm not ashamed of him."

Michael reassured James. "Never be ashamed of your grandfather. This church is all about redemption. I believe Jesus forgave your grandfather like St. Dismas, the Good Thief, was forgiven."

The Bible holds that St. Dismas said to Christ as they were being crucified next to each other: "*Jesus, remember me when you come into your kingdom.*" Although never formally canonized by the Catholic

Church, Christ gave St. Dismas immediate salvation during their crucifixion, saying, "*This day thou shalt be with me in paradise.*"

Further comforting James, Michael reminded him, "Your grandfather did God's work by helping to build that church."

Michael sensed James's relief. He replied, "You're right. I never thought about it that way." Then, Michael added, "You know, your father must have known about the plaque. I don't understand why he didn't tell you. The plaque is memorable."

James shrugged. "Eh, my father didn't say much. When he was dying of emphysema at fifty-three years old, he finally told me some stories. One of the stories was about Vincenzo James, your grandfather, getting murdered and my grandfather being sent away to prison for avenging his older brother."

"All those family members of the older generation were closed-mouth, except for their whispers, like that tale of revenge," Michael said. "I heard that one, too. But there's more to that story than what meets the eye."

Then James dropped a bombshell on Michael. "Actually, I learned some other big parts of my grandfather's past from letters he wrote to my grandmother while in prison. I learned more from the letters than from my dad. They helped me piece together my grandfather's life during his time away."

For Michael, uncovering Uncle Fran's letters was like finding the Holy Grail. While he had learned much about his family's history through archived newspaper stories and conversations with family members, these letters were personal and would add a new dimension to his research. They told the story about Uncle Fran's life on the inside; reading them would be like being a fly on the prison walls.

"How did you get these letters?"

"After my grandmother died, I found them hidden away in a shoebox lined with blue velvet in her closet."

Michael finally got his hands on the box of letters. But not without a little tension. A week after their epic phone conversation, he had met James in the Highlands of New Jersey, where his cousin now lived. When James opened the door to his home, Michael thought about how his cousin, as an older man, looked a lot like Uncle Fran at a similar age. He had the same elongated looks as his grandfather, facially and in his slim figure.

After hugging at the door to seal their new bond, James invited Michael inside his house. "Can I get you something to drink," asked James. "Coffee, Scotch, whatever?" Wanting to loosen up, Michael said, "Scotch is fine."

When James went to the bar in the living room, Michael eyed a photograph of Uncle Fran and Aunt Isabella in a golden frame on top of the china cabinet. He moved in for a closer look to see a picture of Jamesy to the left of his mother and father; on the right side, one of his sister Connie. Transfixed on Connie's portrait, Michael recalled learning of her sudden death from a brain aneurism at a Girl Scout meeting on Long Island during the mid-1960s. The reoccurring dark angels danced past Michael in his head. The image of them then dissolved into memory—of Uncle Fran's rumored reaction when he heard the news by phone at his home: "Why Connie?" he asked, looking up to the ceiling in anguish. "She was a good girl. It should have been me. Why did *You* not take me instead?"

Sensing his Cousin James walking up behind him with the drinks, Michael turned around and broke away from the past. Welcoming the Scotch, he sipped it, happily coming out of that bad memory.

Initially, James did not have the box of letters ready to hand over to Michael. Knowing that Michael had been a journalist, he was ambivalent about giving the letters to him. He wondered if Michael intended to write about the Cimino family's story.

"Let's put our cards on the table," James said. "Do you want the letters because you're planning to write a book about the brothers and our family?" Michael was surprised by James's directness but needed to be honest with his cousin. "Yes, I'm thinking about telling the family's story. I believe it's a blockbuster!" James, not sounding encouraging, countered, "You know my grandmother didn't want the story told."

Michael had to be delicate. "Look, James, I respected the older generation's wishes when they were all alive. I know about that code of silence. But the older family members are all gone now, and I feel compelled to leave this legacy."

Although James's body language still showed some reluctance, he eventually yielded to Michael's persuasiveness. "Okay, I'm on board. But you must know some in the family will be offended by you telling the story."

Michael would not be deterred. "I know exactly

who they are, but I'm taking my shot. I've waited a long time, and now I worry that time is no longer on my side. I'm closer to the end than the beginning."

A hush hung in the air. Michael's strong words silenced his cousin, and all James could do was turn over the box of letters. When Michael received them, he saw they were packaged in chronological order of the dates they were written. The letters would be enlightening, and Michael wanted to patiently read them; every word mattered to him. He did allow himself a quick peek at one letter—the first letter Uncle Fran wrote to Aunt Isabella.

Uncle Fran had arrived at Sing Sing prison after completing the train trip under tight security from Grand Central Station.

The letter focused on his lament about going away and first impressions of the maximum-security prison.

Filled with much emotion, the letter ends with Uncle Fran expressing worry over his brother, Leo.

October 31 1937

Dearest Isabella,

I am so sorry for this nightmare that has caused you pain. When I left Grand Central on the train for Sing Sing with five other prisoners and two deputy sherrifs I could not take my eyes off the pitcher of you and me and our children during happy times.

I love you very much. But I do not know if you should wait for me to be free. May be best to divorce me and start a new life. Living with your sister Millie and raising the kids alone will be tough. The kids need a father. Will see what happens.

First thing I noticed when we got here was the stink. Damn it. The stink seems like what hell must be like. The other guys say its just the smell of all the bad things that happened here. Its everywhere. Just gets under my skin.

Then I was given a uniform. I wear it every day. All the prisoners look the same here. Guess they want to take away our spirit. But I know I must find something I like to do to help kill the time before the time kills me. For now I work in the tailer shop. The work keeps me busy. So I am not always thinkin about gettin outta here.

But I still feel very lonely. I feel the lonelyness all the time and everywhere around me. I feel it when I look at the walls and the soltary and the faces of other men in here.

The lights are going out soon. Darkness makes me feel worst. But tomorrow there will be daylight. That is some small hope.

Take care of yourself and the kids. And please check on my Leo. He is in his own kind of prison.

I love you,

Fran

THIRTEEN

Leo's Addiction

Uncle Leo, alias "Ruby Lips," named for a split upper lip he got in a bar fight, was indeed imprisoned in his own addiction. This was another family secret that had leaked out and was overheard by Michael when he was younger. Morphine had become the wonder drug to relieve pain from post-operative surgery in the 1920s. But by the 1930s, morphine addiction had become a big problem in the country.

On the streets of Coney Island in the mid-1920s, Uncle Leo met a nurse who set his course in life for decades. Her name was Eva Bitten Appel, and she was addicted to morphine and attracted to tattoos. Uncle Leo had tattoos on his chest and shoulders. She turned Uncle Leo on to the drug, which is addictive as heroin. Then they married, and their marriage became convenient. Eva, a real-life TV "Nurse Jackie," stole morphine from the hospital to feed their habit. Michael had heard she'd snuck dope out on a part of her body where no one dared look.

However, by the early 1930s, Uncle Leo had drifted away from Eva because they no longer had morphine in common. They divorced. Uncle Leo had taken the cure and eventually got off the morphine, which Michael read about in a story published in the *Times Reporter of Brooklyn* on November 21, 1932. Almost two months after the arrest during that night of hunting Diamond Dick, this story reported Uncle Leo stood before Judge Robert Baylor in Brooklyn County Court on a misdemeanor charge of gun possession. These were the same weapons the NYPD found when that hunt was intercepted.

Uncle Leo had purportedly begged, "Judge, Your Honor, if you send me to the Island (a prison on Welfare Island, later renamed Roosevelt Island, in the East River) I'm sunk. I was a dope addict, but I took the cure. If I go back to that hole, I'll get on the stuff again. You can't help it when you're on the Island."

According to the story, Uncle Leo had, two weeks earlier, copped a guilty plea to the gun-possession charge. Copping a plea bargained the original felony from the weapons possession rap. The plea bargain to a misdemeanor, however, meant a short sentence at the Welfare Island prison. But Uncle Leo was determined not to go back to the reported "dope ring" island.

"Your Honor," Uncle Leo backpedaled with tears in his eyes, "I want to withdraw my plea and take the rap for a felony."

To Michael, Uncle Leo hadn't appeared so ruthless then. The court was "dumbstruck," as the story stated.

"Do you realize what it means if you plead guilty to the felony?" Judge Baylor had asked. "Do you realize I will be compelled to impose a mandatory sentence of seven years in Sing Sing?"

Uncle Leo, shaking and greatly exaggerating to make his point clear, replied, "I don't care if it's seventy years, at least I can't get the stuff in Sing Sing, Your Honor."

He had convincingly appealed to Judge Baylor's sympathy and gotten his wish. The story concluded that the judge allowed Uncle Leo to plead to a lesser crime of attempting to possess weapons. And that's how Uncle Leo ended up facing three to six at Sing Sing. He was paroled in the spring of 1935.

Night Dreams

After Michael read the story about Uncle Leo figuratively escaping the dope-infested island prison, that night he had a strange dream. He dreamt about sitting around Uncle Fran's kitchen table in Bath Beach, Brooklyn, and listening to a conversation between his dad and uncle.

In Michael's dream, he couldn't take his eyes off one of Uncle Fran's prison paintings. He kept seeing his uncle's painting of a matador alone in a bullring. The seats in the arena were empty. Much of the color in the painting was blood red.

Surely, Michael couldn't know what Uncle Fran was thinking when he painted this picture. Nor could he read the meaning of dreams. But he did see some symbolism. Michael guessed the bullfighter was Uncle Fran fighting off threatening circumstances. And the empty arena meant Uncle Fran was alone without support from those people who'd once applauded him. Finally, he believed the blood red in the painting might have symbolized his uncle's bloody past.

When Michael awoke from the dream, at first, he couldn't remember what his father and Uncle Fran were saying. But the dream soon triggered a memory in the recesses of his mind. He remembered visiting Uncle Fran with his dad sometime in the early 1960s and a conversation they had about Uncle Leo. As a youngster, Michael was precocious and a curious listener.

"How's Uncle Leo?" his dad, Nicky, asked.

"He's clean from the drugs and living in Vermont."

"But why was Uncle Leo on drugs for so many years?"

Michael recalled Uncle Fran had replied, "Kicking his addiction for good had been nearly impossible. When a user first finds and likes a particular drug, it's a great relief. But addiction gets increasingly painful and is a dead end. I'll tell you a story that still haunts me. One night, Leo came knocking on my door before I went away to Sing Sing. I was on the lam at the time because of that murder charge. Not many people knew where to find me then. Well, when I opened the door, he stood there twitching and scratching himself and screaming about bugs biting him. He needed a fix and couldn't scrape together enough money to buy a bag in Coney Island. He was completely physically and psychologically addicted. He needed morphine just to feel normal."

Michael, immersed in the memory, had to dig deep to remember more.

"So, did you give him the money?" Nicky asked.

"I'd been giving him money for years to feed his habit. This night, he wanted to kick it on his own—cold turkey and no hospital. I rocked him like a baby for three days and kept him warm with blankets; it takes at least three days to get the monkey off your back—to free your soul. Three days of agony. But Leo, once again, had kicked the habit. Then he went back on the morphine like clockwork. It was only a matter of time. He was a junkie."

FOURTEEN
Who Rode the Lightning?

Getting back to real-time from the memory of that early 1960s conversation about Uncle Leo, Michael discovered perhaps the darkest of twists to his family's dangerous past. The discovery initially stemmed from another newspaper story about two early arrests of Uncle Leo. And as Michael studied his family tree again, coupled with the revelation from this newspaper article, a death in the electric chair became clear to him.

The family tree showed that Maria Elena, mother to actor Frankie Fortunato, had been married to a man named Giuseppe Stefano before she'd married Frankie's father, Francisco Fortunato. While Michael had overlooked this connection between Maria Elena and Giuseppe at first glance of the family tree, his eye for detail caught it the next time. Maria Elena's marriage to her first husband, which resulted in their only daughter being born, was short-lived. According to the tree, Giuseppe died in 1932. But how did he die? It would be an electrifying discovery, so to speak. How Michael learned about what had happened was especially quirky.

He turned again to Big Marcio to help with the detective work. At the time, Big Marcio was the only person alive, known to Michael, who had a strong pulse on the Cimino family's past. He might have the scoop. So, Michael called the man.

"Hey, Big, it's Michael Cimino. I'm still researching the Cimino brothers' past, and I spotted a connection on the family tree, along with an old newspaper article, that has raised questions. Something just doesn't fit."

Responding, Big Marcio said, "Whadaya got?"

"I noticed on my family tree that Maria Elena Cimino Fortunato, my grandfather's sister, was first married to a Giuseppe Stefano. But Giuseppe passed away shortly after Maria Elena gave birth to their baby girl. Do you know anything more about this?"

Big Marcio knew the scuttlebutt and quickly shared it. "The rumor is that a shotgun wedding took place just prior to the start of the 1920s. Maria Elena got pregnant, and she consequently had to marry Giuseppe. I believe the baby was named Jolanda."

He was right about the baby's name. The family tree confirmed her name.

Continuing their conversation, Big Marcio said, "The Stefanos were just as dangerous as the Ciminos and helped influence the three brothers' delinquent behavior. Maria Elena, who was on the wild side like her brothers, relished running with gangsters." He paused for a moment, then added, "That's all I got for you right now. Figure the rest out on your own. We'll talk again another time."

"But what about—" Michael started to ask, but then quickly realized Big Marcio was no longer listening. The conversation had already ended.

Michael went on a mission, first getting back to studying the tree. During Maria Elena's second marriage to Francisco Fortunato, she gave birth to her only boy who grew up to be the famous actor. She also had four other girls with Francisco. Michael wondered whether all the siblings remained close with half-sister Jolanda. Only Maria Elena could be the link to keep them all together, he guessed.

Most significant to Michael, the tree showed that Jolanda had married Anthony Winston. He integrated the only Waspy connection to the Italians on the tree. And the couple had a son called Tony, who later became an interesting source of information for Michael. He, in fact, created the ancestry chart named the "Winston Family Tree," although the tree mostly featured members of the Cimino family—ancestors going back to Naples, Italy, and descendants later born in America. Overall, the tree included extended families of the Winstons, Ciminos, Fortunatos, and Prisinzanos.

The Prisinzanos entered the family when Dorinda Cimino, baby of the Cimino siblings, married Pasquale Prisinzano. Pasquale ran an ice-delivery business in Brooklyn where crime boss Frankie Yale had controlled the industry. For Pasquale, ice delivery turned into owning and operating five private sanitation trucks, which were inherited by his children. After decades of operating the family business, the trucks were sold outside the Prisinzano family.

Family connections demonstrated that the tree undoubtedly had dark roots. But one connection appeared especially dark and twisted to Michael because of how he put the pieces together.

The Winston Family Tree and a small newspaper story about Uncle Leo's early arrests were a one-two combination that struck Michael hard. However, this discovery all about Giuseppe Stefano and his death seemed off kilter.

Studying the *Brooklyn Daily Flyer* story of June 23, 1922, Michael learned about Uncle Leo getting arrested and charged for two separate crimes in Brooklyn. One for threatening and assaulting a man at Williamsburg Bridge Plaza and another for assault and robbery with five other men about six months earlier on Christmas Day.

But it was this side note to the story's angle that was most compelling. The note reported that Uncle Leo was the brother-in-law to Frank Stefano, who was on death row at Sing Sing. Although just one sentence, this minor mention stuck out to Michael more than the news of Uncle Leo's crimes itself. Further research revealed Stefano was waiting to get the electric chair for murdering a man at Richmond Hill on Staten Island.

But based on the tree, Michael recognized Uncle Leo's only brother-in-law named Stefano—through his sister Maria Elena—was Giuseppe.

Was the reported Frank Stefano and genealogy-charted Giuseppe Stefano the same person? Michael's instincts suggested they were indeed and that the paper had gotten the first name wrong. What other solution could there be? The *Flyer* story, which connected Uncle Leo to the Stefano on death row, had run on June 23, 1922. Therefore, Stefano conceivably might have died in the electric chair the following year in 1923—the year indicating the death of twenty-four-year-old Giuseppe Stefano on the family tree.

Not fully satisfied, Michael researched further, to

document his detective work. Searching the internet once again, he discovered Stefano's Sing Sing prison record. Four key facts showed up on his record:

Number one, his first name was listed as Joseph—not Frank. Joseph was the Americanization of Giuseppe.

Second, his conviction showed murder in the first degree with a term of execution, which meant the electric chair.

Third, his wife's name was noted as Mary, the English form of Marie. And that's shortened for Maria Elena.

Finally, the record verified his occupation as marble cutter, a trade he mostly likely learned, like the Cimino brothers, from his father-in-law, Giuseppe Cimino.

Michael now believed the facts proved his instincts were right—case closed. One mystery down, but more to go, it seemed to him.

FIFTEEN

Inside Story

While the pieces for solving Giuseppe Stefano's mysterious death fell into place for Michael, his grandfather's disappearance was still relatively a cold case. He was getting warmer with each new discovery but needed some solid answers to finally crack it. He hoped Uncle Fran's letters written to Aunt Isabella from prison might provide clues to solving the case once and for all … or at least get him very close to the final resolution. Unlike getting the story from old newspaper articles, conversations with family members, and ancient documents, these letters would offer unique insight into his uncle's perspective.

Just before Uncle Fran left Sing Sing for the notorious Dannemora up in the North Country, he wrote one last letter. It was upbeat, expressing his positivity over a *new beginning* at Dannemora.

March 20 1939

Dearest Isabella,

Today is the first day of spring. Tommorow Im on my way to Dannemora. I hear the inmates call this place little Siberia. I know the weather there is colder than Sing Sing. But at least it is spring now so the tempertur there will not be a big shock.

The change should be a new beginning. Looking foward to building this church on the prison grounds. The priest who got the idea to build it wants the best stone masons. I heard the construction will be all stone. Looks like knowing the trade should benefit me in prison. And the church will benefit the inmates.

You know the word here is that Charlie Luciano is at Dannemora. Wonder if he will get involved with the church. I have not seen him since 1931. Funny that after all these years we end up in the same place together. And its crazy the church is bringing us together.

Will see what happens when we meet. That will be intrusting.

Love,

Fran

For Uncle Fran, reforms that followed the 1929 riots at Dannemora meant a sense of freedom in prison through art. New indoor recreation allowed prisoners various outlets, including the fine art of painting.

Uncle Fran played the mandolin and was a stone and marble mason. His hands were an instrument for creativity and building. His talents, combined with a need to fill his heart and soul with something to pass the time, led him to picking up an artist's brush.

Michael's hand fell upon another letter, and he moved it closer so he could read it again. It was telling, filled with sentimentality, and Michael was touched at the passion that existed in his great-uncle—for better or for worse.

December 1, 1939

Dearest Isabella,

Today is the anniversary of my brother's death. Looking back, I have many emotions. I'm sad. I'm happy for times that we were all young brothers to-gether in Brooklyn. And I still feel the vengeance. Seems like such a long time ago.

But writing to you helps me to get over the bad emotions. And you may notice that my writing has greatly improved. Father Hyland, who is leading the way in building the church here, is helping me to write better. I never spoke about it, but I always regretted not getting past middle school. That's just the way it was being Italian and growing up in Brooklyn back then. I'm trading some of my paint-ings to him in exchange for his help. He's a big lover of art.

Guess you're wondering about the painting. Well, I'm learning to paint pictures. Just seems to be a natural talent of mine. They call me van Gogh here.

I just completed my painting of a matador in a bull-ring. One of my cellmates, Albert Cruz, told me about seeing the bullfights in Mexico. He described the bullfighting so clearly. I pictured the scene in my mind.

Now I'm working on a new painting. The painting is a portrait of my brothers and me. The night we were all together in Coney Island doing that big job for Maranzano in 1931 inspired the painting. I'm going to paint us all in black. That was a dark night.

Will get back to painting now. It's a way to help do the time.

Looking forward to hearing from you soon, Isa-bella.

Love,

Fran

Since Uncle Fran's transfer from Sing Sing to Dannemora, life on the inside became more tolerable, it seemed. Between Uncle Fran cutting and setting stone to build the Church of St. Dismas and painting pictures, he became absorbed in the work. The routine of prison life was reforming Uncle Fran; there was a diametric difference between his controlled attitude and behavior on the inside and his explosive nature on the outside, along Brooklyn's streets. He felt a newfound hope.

At the center of his optimism was Father Hyland. The Father encouraged Uncle Fran's painting and his work building the church. The priest and his protégé were bonding in a special way.

Father Hyland even helped to reunite Uncle Fran with Luciano.

March 15, 1940

Dearest Isabella,

The calendar shows that today is the Ides of March. I learned in prison that Julius Caesar was double crossed and assassinated on this day. The day reminds me that I'm around an old enemy, Lucky Luciano. We've met again through Father Hyland. I'll soon tell you what happened.

First, I want to say that the Father has become a good friend. He is motivating me to paint. The more

I paint the better I feel. And he always praises my work building the church. Helping to build the church brings me great satisfaction. The church is changing the lives of many prisoners. When we complete it, they can come here for peace.

The Father brought Luciano to look at the church's construction—and we've met. I hear that Luciano is donating money to help build the church. Don't know how the money specifically is being used on the church. But this is a smart move for him. He's always been clever. I'm sure he's trying to rebuild his image after all the bad press over the years. Luciano approached me. I had my guard up. He wanted both of us to sit down and clear the air. Of course, we had a couple of neutral inmates with us. Still, I didn't know if I could trust him. But I had to know what he wanted to say. So, I agreed.

Luciano believed the score was settled. He said James had to be taken out by his order because my brother was too ambitious. He insisted it was not personal but felt threatened that James would have stood in his way. Luciano had taken over everything in Brooklyn and Manhattan, and he thought James might turn on him.

In his view, I had evened the score when I avenged James by cutting up Di Marco with my dagger and ending him by putting it through his heart. Riccardo was the godson of Luciano's father. In any case, it's over now, so best we bury it.

Hug the kids for me. I miss you all very much.

Love,

Fran

A few months after the Church of St. Dismas was

dedicated in late August of 1941, the Japanese attack on Pearl Harbor shocked the nation on December 7th of that same year. "A day that will live in infamy," the iconic lament of President Franklin D. Roosevelt, was heard around the world, including cell blocks of Dannemora.

Building and opening a church behind prison walls for the first time in the country represented a place of peace for Dannemora's inmates. The attack on Pearl Harbor meant the opposite. War was looming. But inmates in all prisons across the nation were insulated from the next big war, and prisoners could not participate in fighting for their country.

Uncle Fran, however, knew about the violence of war. He was in the middle of the Castellammarese War of 1931, the bloody turf battle between rival Italian crime factions from Brooklyn and Manhattan. The violence in that war could be likened to any world war, only across a smaller geographic landscape. In the end, all wars are about power, money and control.

It was clear to Michael that Uncle Fran embraced peace more than war while at Dannemora. The Church of St. Dismas was a place of serenity, and he was emotionally connected to it.

December 8, 1941

Dearest Isabella,

The prison guards have passed the word around about the Japanese attack on Pearl Harbor yesterday. We're hearing the news secondhand from them, so I don't know the full emotion of what you're feeling at home. Japs pulled off a big double cross. I suppose this attack means war.

Being on the inside, my cellmates and I are removed from what's going on at home and around the world. Being isolated I choose to find peace.

I can find peace at the Church of St. Dismas, which opened in August. There are some interesting stories about building the church that I haven't told you. You know Luciano donated that money I once mentioned to buy oak wood to build the pews. Maybe he thinks he'll get a special pardon from God.

And I heard that a descendant of the explorer Magellan gave two carvings of angels to the church. The carvings were found on Magellan's ship that sank in the Philippines in the early 1500s.

But the most interesting story of all is about a convicted forger at Dannemora. He knows how to make stained glass. His name is Carmelo Soraci, and he made stained-glass windows for the church. Especially unusual, Soraci used the inmates as models for his images on the windows. He's a special kind of artist.

Let me know any news about the war in your next letter. And I will write back about how the church is changing morale here.

Love,

Fran

In late 1942, Uncle Fran had received a crushing letter from his wife. In it, Aunt Isabella wrote that she had met another man and needed to move on with her life. She asked for a divorce and wanted to marry again.

Michael winced from the pain he imagined Uncle Fran had felt upon reading the request. And he thought about the Greeney character in *Gates of Dannemora;* how Uncle Fran's new reality resembled Greeney's narrative.

Nevertheless, after reading Uncle Fran's response, Michael was struck by the man's ability to control his emotions in a level-headed manner.

December 24, 1942

Dearest Isabella,

It's Christmas Eve and this time of year is for giving. I would love to be home giving Christmas presents to James and Connie. But I cannot think of what is best for me now.

Understand that I have mixed feelings. While I want to see you free, I also do not want to let you go. But I will give you the divorce that you requested in your last letter. I hope your new man will be good to the children.

I have regrets about my actions in the past. I'm especially sorry we did that job for Maranzano in 1931. I believe that job set off a bad chain of events. But I cannot take anything back. The best I can do now is to involve myself in positive work at Dannemora. Part of that work means trying to shorten my sentence.

I wish you and the children my very best. I love them. I still love you.

Fran

Uncle Fran's letter granting the divorce was the

last one he sent to Aunt Isabella from Dannemora. Subsequently, the once-married couple was officially divorced and no longer communicating. The physical separation and adjustment to prison life when Uncle Fran initially was *sent up the river* seemed bitter, as bemoaned in his first letter from Sing Sing. But the finality of being divorced could only have doubled the emotional pain. And knowing Uncle Fran would probably not be seeing James and Connie until his release likely exasperated what he was feeling. To put everything into perspective: by the time Uncle Fran expected his release from Dannemora, his children would have grown to be adults.

SIXTEEN

Just Like Bonnie and Clyde

The person now closest to Uncle Fran, both geo-graphically and through blood, was his brother Leo. He had been living in Canada, a car ride away from Dannemora, while Uncle Fran was at the peniten-tiary. Michael had known, from the time he was a young man, that Uncle Leo had spent time in Canada. He had heard about his uncle crossing the northern border around the same time he learned of Uncle Fran's prison term. The two brothers' history had been linked, and there always had been veiled talk about Uncle Leo, too.

Growing up, the family's younger generation, in-cluding Michael, wondered about Uncle Leo's moti-vation for moving to Canada. During the midst of Michael's research, the reason for Uncle Leo fleeing across the border finally dawned on him. He sur-mised that after Uncle Fran was convicted of the lesser manslaughter offense for killing John DeVito, Uncle Leo feared that members of the DeVito family might retaliate against him.

Michael believed the DeVitos, encouraged by Judge Bragante's outspoken opinion, felt that full justice had not been served. The DeVito brood surely was expecting a conviction of first-degree murder ra-ther than Uncle Fran's lesser manslaughter convic-tion that resulted in a shorter sentence. Anything short of the death penalty or, at least, life in prison had to have been an affront to that family. Although paranoia is a symptom of drug addiction, Uncle Leo's fear was real. In fact, Big Marcio confirmed everything Michael had surmised.

Living in Montreal, Canada, Uncle Leo met Rachel Gale Briggs, who just happened to be a nurse. Sound familiar? Certainly, it all seemed familiar to Michael. He had heard the rumors about Rachel many years earlier, just as he had listened to the whispers of Eva Bitten Appel, the nurse Uncle Leo met in Coney Island and later married, then divorced. Plus, seeing that Rachel was married to Uncle Leo on the Winston Family Tree made the story real to him. Apparently, Uncle Leo liked nurses—and for good reason. They worked where drugs could be found. Their joining up together, sometime between 1942 and 1943, was like pairing the infamous Bonnie Parker with her bank-robber boyfriend, Clyde Barrow.

One big difference: Uncle Leo and Rachel had been using drugs throughout their crime spree. They both were addicted to heroin and morphine. And their addiction motivated the robberies. Uncle Leo had corrupted his female companion, starting her on the "stuff," as the chronic addict once described the dope to Brooklyn County Court Judge Baylor. Like Uncle Leo's first encounter with a nurse in Coney Island all those years ago, Rachel stole drugs from the hospital to feed their habit. Uncle Leo had taught her the ropes. That was the rumor Michael had heard growing up, and he leaned toward believing it.

Between stealing drugs from the hospital and robbing people on the streets in Montreal to buy their narcotics, Uncle Leo and Rachel had a baby boy in

1944. They had not yet married. Michael learned about the boy, named "Little" Leo, from a 1947 newspaper story about Thanksgiving Day generosity from the NYPD.

Two years prior to that Thanksgiving Day, Uncle Leo brought Rachel and the baby back to Brooklyn. The dust had settled, and his fear of the DeVito family had dissipated. That same year, Uncle Leo and Rachel married on June 15, 1945. Michael discovered the date from their marriage license, which showed up on the internet.

For the next two years of the marriage, the couple reportedly survived financially and attempted to get clean from the drugs. Uncle Leo had been working in construction, but he injured his back on the job, as reported in later news stories about welfare corruption. Unable to work, Uncle Leo hit hard times. That was when the NYPD came to lend a hand, rather than add another arrest to Uncle Leo's long rap sheet.

According to a news story in the *Brooklyn Daily Flyer*, which published November 28, 1947, there was no food in the Cimino household on Thanksgiving Day. Uncle Leo, now forty-seven years old, ironically went running *to* the NYPD rather than *away*. The story noted, he appeared "coatless, shivering and hesitant in front of the Sheepshead Bay police station" on Thanksgiving Day.

Upon reading the article, Michael immediately felt sorry for Uncle Leo; in fact, tears had started to well.

According to the story, Uncle Leo gathered his courage and "approached Detective Walton Lowry standing on the station house steps." Detective

Lowry invited Uncle Leo into the station, and Michael's hapless uncle explained that his family had nothing to eat.

Detective Lowry then collaborated with two high-ranking police officers about finding food for the Cimino family. They called neighborhood store owners to convince them to open their doors, despite having the holiday off. The storekeepers rose to the occasion and rounded up assorted foods, including turkey dinners, veal, cold cuts, a large bag of potatoes, and other vegetables as well as various fruits. The detective had even added some toys, the story reported, and delivered the stockpile with his fellow officers to the Cimino Coney Island home.

The article ended with Rachel, "her lips quivering," saying, "'Thank you, thank you.'"

Overall, the *Brooklyn Daily Flyer* story seemed bittersweet, especially after seeing the photo and caption that ran with the full piece. The newspaper spread depicted a down-on-their-luck family at their home with Detective Lowry and one of the officers handing them a turkey dinner that Thanksgiving Day.

Examining the photo, Michael, on the surface, saw an all-American family. Uncle Leo, dressed up in his suit and tie, was holding three-year-old Little Leo in his lap. And Rachel, a pretty lady in a flowered dress, was feeding milk to the couple's newest child—one-year-old Francesco sitting in a highchair. The baby evidently was named after his Uncle Fran, who still was doing time at Dannemora prison. Michael wondered how many of the newspaper's readers knew about the Cimino family's criminal past.

Bad Backs and Kickbacks

The backstory that Michael had read about the beleaguered Bonnie and Clyde-like couple was printed in the *New York Daily Press* on Saturday of that Thanksgiving Day weekend.

The headline: "Refused Kick-back, Lost Relief, He Says."

According to the story, Uncle Leo said he had lost his monthly welfare relief check of $124.70. Since September 1945, he had been receiving the money due to injuring his back on a construction job.

The article reported that Uncle Leo observed a lady welfare investigator had called him to explain "he wasn't entitled to relief because he was drawing $100 a month compensation insurance." Uncle Leo protested that his compensation went toward paying his medical bills. But he claimed the investigator said, "Well, I know how hard it is to get along. We're all working people. I can use a gift every month and you would get your check." To Michael, she sounded like a con conning the con, proving there really was *no honor* among thieves.

The story stated the woman requested $24.70 a month from Uncle Leo. This amount of money nowadays seemed small, of course, but back in the day … not so small. Uncle Leo told the investigator he "wouldn't payoff." Michael gave him credit for sticking to his guns and not giving in to the woman's demands. As a result, Uncle Leo claimed, he was dropped from the welfare relief.

According to the news article, Uncle Leo charged the woman with wanting a kickback.

Welfare Commissioner Ben Friedman, in fact, reportedly had dismissed one department investigator for either seeking or taking money from people on relief.

The story of Uncle Leo's kickback charge reached as far as Ontario, Canada. Michael suspected that since Uncle Leo and his wife had lived near that part of Canada and probably had been infamously known there, their latest controversy made news in Ontario.

The *Windsor Sun* (Windsor, Ontario) published a story on December 2, 1947 about Brooklyn probing this relief graft case. The article said the Brooklyn district attorney's office started an investigation on charges that the Ciminos "falsely accused a female welfare relief investigator of demanding a gift out of their monthly check."

But the story concluded the Cimino case was turned over to welfare's Commissioner of Investigations Jack Murphy, whose decision was not in favor of Uncle Leo and Rachel. The commissioner determined the duo's charge against the female worker was false; therefore, she was exonerated. The justification was that the commissioner believed the Ciminos hadn't reported the $100-a-month income from workmen's compensation, which tested their credibility.

However, Michael sensed some inconsistency to the story. The *Windsor Sun* reported the commissioner had announced a "sweeping personnel program" for New York City's relief administration, filling 698 vacancies on the staff. He said the new employees would be chosen from a list of 2,000 social investigators supplied by the Municipal Civil Service Commission.

To Michael, all these widespread personnel changes should have lent credence to Uncle Leo's graft charge against the female welfare investigator. Somehow it did not, and this left Michael raising his eyebrow in doubt.

Reversal of Fortune

The duo's streak of bad times, mostly instigated by the couple, continued until a strange twist of fate happened. Just over four years later, there was another article telling of the NYPD chasing down a man and woman believed to be "narcotics addicts" and involved with a partner who was shot dead by a rookie cop. The shooting occurred after the threesome held up a man on New York City's East Side, according to the *Brooklyn Daily Flyer* story published on April 14, 1952.

The headline: "Thug Slain, Police Hunt Two in Holdup." Reportedly, charges of assault and robbery with a gun were filed against Leo Cimino, alias Ruby Lips, and his forty-two-year-old, brunette wife, Rachel, a.k.a. "Cimino." Just like Bonnie and Clyde, the infamous pair kept adding to their rap sheet.

Based on the story, police said the drug-addicted couple and fifty-year-old Walter Clarke held up a rent collector named Karol Kutowski. Pointing a gun with blanks at the man, the threesome pulled off the hold-up for only thirty dollars. But the small-time robbery turned into a big-time incident when a chase for the threesome ended with Clarke getting shot and killed by the cop.

Unexpectedly, the story reported, Kutowski died of natural causes in New York City's Bellevue prison ward. Turned out Kutowski also had been involved with drugs and was being held on narcotics charges. His death resulted just before he was about to testify against the Ciminos, who were charged with assault and robbery with a gun.

The twist? While two men had died, Uncle Leo and his wife won a dismissal of the criminal charges because Kutowski could no longer testify.

This, too, had Michael shaking his head, but this time with muddled admiration. The couple had gone from unlucky to lucky in the blink of an eye.

Many years later, Uncle Leo apparently attempted to redeem himself while living in Burlington, Vermont. *The Burlington Record* reported he had saved a Siamese cat from a burning apartment house in Burlington on July 26, 1961. The fire was a three-alarm blaze that forced twenty-nine people out of the building.

Uncle Leo's rescue of the cat was really brave and honorable. But those positive vibes would eventually end. From death certificates found on the internet, Michael learned Rachel had died from asphyxiation in Burlington on August 6, 1964, and Uncle Leo succumbed to pneumonia fourteen years later in Burlington on October 10, 1978.

Throughout his life, Michael never had any contact with Uncle Leo and his wife or their two boys. To him, they were all ghosts of the past, only known through family whispers, a family tree, and old newspaper stories and other records.

Such an odd couple, Michael thought. Whenever he pictured the pair raising hell on the streets, Bonnie and Clyde came to mind.

SEVENTEEN

Free as a Bird

Sixteen months after Uncle Leo and his wife, Rachel, experienced their reversal of fortune, Uncle Fran also had a change of luck. He would be saying goodbye to Dannemora! After spending sixteen years in prison, Uncle Fran was officially released from Little Siberia on August 19, 1953. The number "16" that linked the brothers, coupled with their similar luck, seemed to be another anomaly.

Michael, who never missed a beat, noted the oddity. And it further colored the story of Uncle Fran's release, which Michael had learned from his dad soon after meeting his uncle in 1959. However, he didn't know details prompting the release. His ignorance was about to change.

The former reporter had discovered another *New York Daily Press* story, published the day after Uncle Fran's release, that explained how his uncle was freed. He read this article and felt now it was time to share the full story with Cousin James. Michael hadn't before because he didn't want to paint a poor picture of Uncle Fran, but he just couldn't hold back the truth about his manslaughter conviction any longer.

Michael arranged another meeting with his cousin in the Highlands of New Jersey. This time he brought copies of all the newspaper clippings and other documents about the Cimino family, so James could see the facts for himself, changing the folklore. Michael believed his gesture would help to return the favor for receiving Uncle Fran's prison letters from James.

As Michael handed the papers to his cousin, he said, "I learned much of the truth about your grandfather from these old newspaper stories and records. Do you want me to tell you what I know, then you can read for yourself later?"

James replied, "Yes, tell me everything. I need to know what really happened."

Like everyone from the family's younger generation, James had only heard the whispers. After Michael explained the real reason Uncle Fran was sent away, James was awed. Hearing the folklore for so long seemed to have made it the truth, but now the curtain had been torn away—and the reality was stunning to James.

Michael particularly held up the *Daily Press* article. "According to this story, your grandfather was released from Dannemora on August 19, 1953, because he had been wrongfully sentenced. This Judge Bragante gave your grandfather thirty years for a first-degree manslaughter conviction, tacking on an extra ten years for being a second offender. But your grandfather was improperly represented for this prior third-degree robbery charge."

James then asked, "What led the court to shorten my grandfather's sentence?"

"Your grandfather had always been convinced he didn't get lawful representation during the robbery trial, just as the *Daily Press* reported," Michael said. "So, he kept fighting for fairness. But, reportedly,

your dad—who had hardly remembered your grandfather from his early childhood—actually served as
the catalyst to free him."

James, surprised that his father had put the release in motion, replied, "My father never said a
word. How did he help get my grandfather out?"

"Apparently, your father, a navy man at the time,
got the Red Cross interested in helping to get your
grandfather's case reviewed. The Red Cross then appealed to Kings County Court Judge Lewis Golden,
who passed the case on to attorney Nathaniel Shore
to probe. Shore found out your grandfather was improperly represented by his counsel at the robbery
trial. So, Judge Golden granted a writ of error and
corrected the court's mistake. After throwing out the
first robbery offense, the judge determined your
grandfather had served enough time on the manslaughter charge—which should have been a ten- to
twenty-year sentence—and so he freed your grandfather."

For James, the truth had set him free, too, it
seemed—based on what Michael could tell from his
cousin's expression. The weight of wondering all
those years about what happened with his grandfather had finally been lifted. But James wanted to
know more about how it all went down during the
day of Uncle Fran's release.

So, Michael referred to the *Daily Press* article
he'd held up earlier, underscoring and explaining
parts of it to his cousin. And James, observing the
photo with the story, now saw for himself his father,
in a sailor uniform, shaking hands with Judge
Golden. He gazed at the image of his grandfather,

dressed in a suit and necktie and looking very handsome, standing between the other men and smiling ear-to-ear. With his arm around his son, Uncle Fran appeared to have come a long way from wearing a prison uniform. He was on the road back.

Still questioning, it seemed James needed every detail to satisfy himself. "How did my grandfather react when he heard about being freed from Dannemora?"

"When you read the full article, you'll understand the roller coaster of his emotions," Michael said. "But here's the short story ... He showed emotions that quickly changed. Your grandfather had blinked a little uncomprehendingly when he heard the law had erred and that he was now a free man. Then Judge Golden's words of freedom hit home. Your grandfather both cried and laughed with joy."

Finally, James raised the question that could not be ignored: "Where was my grandmother when my grandfather learned about his freedom?"

"Your grandmother was there, James, according to the story. When your grandfather heard about getting released, he turned to reunite with your father and grandmother. And your grandfather looked proudly at your grandmother and announced they would remarry soon."

James replied, "I knew my grandfather and grandmother divorced when he was at Dannemora. I read the letter that my grandfather wrote to my grandmother from prison. But what did my grandmother do after the divorce? From the letter, I know she was seeing someone, but nobody in the family spoke about that period in her life."

"The topic was taboo around the family," Michael said. "The *Daily Press* story explains a little. In the article, your grandmother was referred to as Isabella Cimino Savante, as Michael pointed for James to see. After the divorce, your grandmother evidently married a man named Savante."

"What happened to him?"

"He died in 1946, according to a follow-up *Daily Press* story that reported your grandfather and grandmother remarrying. Judge Golden, in fact, remarried them, as he had promised earlier. After his promise, he said to your grandfather, 'I'm convinced you'll become a useful citizen, and so are the warden and chaplain at Dannemora.'"

A good life on the outside seemed to be beginning for Uncle Fran. As Father Hyland once said, "Men in prison can come back."

EIGHTEEN

Second Time Around

Uncle Fran went back in time by remarrying Aunt Isabella, but he was approaching their future with hope. After Uncle Fran's release from Dannemora, the follow-up story in the *Daily Press* described this fortunate day like waking up from a bad dream.

The article, published August 26, 1953, featured the happy headline: "Knot Retied, 16-Year Nightmare Is Over."

The story reported that Uncle Fran appeared in the chambers of Kings County Judge Golden. He was "making his marriage vows for the second time with a brunette" before the judge. Examining the story's photo, Michael, always observant, saw that the passing years had changed Aunt Isabella's figure. Described as once petite by family members, she now looked a little plumper. But the connection between Michael's aunt and uncle went beyond their physical attraction. They had a history and shared their children and extended family.

Uncle Fran's son, Jamesy, stood by watching with pride. Michael imagined that he was likely thinking about how much he'd helped make that joyous day happen. He had a twenty-day leave from the United States Navy, the story reported. The long leave allowed him to savor some family time, which had been lost over the last sixteen years.

From this moment, it was all about catching up and looking ahead. Uncle Fran and Aunt Isabella were planning their second honeymoon, and after that, they'd settle down at their Bath Beach home in Brooklyn. That was where Michael had first met his aunt and uncle as a youngster—the time he had observed his uncle's paintings on the walls, which made an instant and lasting impression. And he could not stop wondering about the mystery of those lost paintings, just couldn't get it out of his head. *Some of those paintings that Uncle Fran traded to Father Hyland may be buried somewhere in the cellar of St. Dismas Church,* Michael dreamed.

But the church that rose from the ground at Dannemora, with the help of his uncle's hands, was in the past now for Uncle Fran. He would be thinking about his future with a new lease on life, though with some adjustments to make.

NINETEEN

Period of Adjustment

While Uncle Fran was now a free man, he still had pent up anger from being imprisoned. According to what Cousin James had shared with Michael during their last meeting in the Highlands, Uncle Fran's explosive nature reared its head on a hot summer night in a Bath Beach bar. Shortly after getting re-married, he was a having a beer with his son, Jamesy. Surely, the navy man was enjoying his extended leave and father's freedom. This night was a "welcome home" party for Uncle Fran. Older people in the neighborhood knew the man and gravitated to him. They all heard his incredible story. He was a local celebrity.

"On that memorable night," noted James, "a young, connected hood approached my grandfather and insulted and provoked him." To use a Hollywood Western analogy, the young gun in the neighborhood appeared to be testing the older gunslinger. The young hood later became known as "Sammy the Sheik."

"So how exactly did this Sheik character test him?" Michael asked.

"Getting under my grandfather's skin, Sammy whispered in his ear, 'What was it like being locked away, knowing that your wife would be divorcing you while seeing another man?' Well, my grandfather exploded, knocking Sammy on his ass and putting the barrel of a 38-caliber in his mouth."

When Michael heard this, he had thought, *some things never change, and Uncle Fran was still carrying*.

"So, what happened next?" he'd asked his cousin with bated breath.

"My father told me he pulled my grandfather off Sammy. He got my grandfather to cool off, and then they left the bar to avoid reigniting the incident."

Thirty Years Later: 1983

During a resurgence of Brooklyn gangsters, Sammy the Sheik had recovered his respect. He had risen in the Colombo crime family ranks and became popular around the neighborhood.

Continuing with a sequel to the story, James spoke of Sammy's second meeting with his father. "All these years after the gun-in-your-mouth episode, in the same Bath Beach bar, my father side-eyed Sammy, vaguely recognizing him. Well, Sammy, who was sitting at a table with his bodyguard, sees my father staring at him. So, he sends his bodyguard to bring my dad to his table."

Blowing smoke rings from his cigar, Michael remarked, "Sounds like this story didn't end well."

"Surprisingly, Sammy actually put out the red carpet for my father after some game-playing. Sammy asked, 'Do you know me?' And my father replied, 'Maybe. Do you know me?'"

Jamesy apparently was playing coy, as the exchange had developed into a cat-and-mouse game.

His son, James, continued. "Then, Sammy eye-balled my father and paused for a double-take. With a half-smile, he said, 'You're the sailor!' Remembering how my father may have saved him from my grandfather, he added, 'Let me know if there's anything I can ever do for you.' But their relationship ended there; my father would not take the bait. He refused to get sucked in and owe any favors. My father learned from my grandfather, who slowly accepted getting out of that violent life."

Just Say No

At Uncle Fran's next crossroads of adjusting to the outside, he was tempted to get back into the life. But when push came to shove, he just said, "No."

Like Terry Molloy's character in *On the Waterfront*, a groundbreaking 1954 film because of its realism about corruption on the docks, Uncle Fran was offered a cushiony dockworker's job. But he declined the offer, as rumored. Coincidentally, Uncle Fran was offered the job about the same time the film opened in movie theaters. It was an example of life imitating art.

Family rumor circulated that the ex-convict, teetering on being tempted, would have to exchange the payoff for cooperating with those thugs who controlled the corruption. He only had to report to the docks, sign in, go home, and get paid. But signing on to the sham job, as similarly alluded to in the film classic, would be like making a *devil's bargain*.

Uncle Fran, who understood the deal's pitfalls, slowly was committing to becoming a useful citizen since his release from Dannemora. Saying "no" to the bogus job offer was, for him, taking a step closer in his adjustment to living a *straight* life.

Hollywood Comes Knocking

The story of Uncle Fran and his brothers, highlighted with building the Church of St. Dismas, was made for Hollywood. But Uncle Fran was conflicted over seeing his story on the big screen and staying under the radar to avoid dredging up his family's dark past for everyone to see—though he had experienced some redemption building the church.

Turning the story into a great film had to start with the screenplay. And the legendary director Billy Wilder wanted to write it and direct the movie. Michael learned about Wilder's interest through family tree creator Tony Winston, who reached out to Michael by phone to expand on the tree. Tony, Frankie Fortunato's nephew through Grandmother Maria Elena, surely had some stories to tell about his Hollywood uncle.

But first he affirmed, in a shrouded way, the story about his grandfather's execution at Sing Sing when Michael brought up this skeleton in the closet. After everything came out, the actor dominated the conversation between the two men, and Tony revealed some rarely told tales about him. "Well, I'll tell you a story I know firsthand. Uncle Frankie landed a job helping to cast *The Seven-Year Itch*, director Billy Wilder's 1954 film starring Marilyn Monroe. He even casted me in a crowd scene with Marilyn. I was nine years old and couldn't keep my eyes off her."

The story certainly fascinated Michael. But

mostly he was curious about how Frankie got that casting job with such a high-profile film, especially since he was new to Hollywood. Michael had an idea, of course, that Frankie's good luck was connected to Father Hyland. Tony's version of what happened confirmed Michael's suspicion. "If you're wondering how Uncle Frankie got the casting job that kicked off his acting career in Hollywood, you can thank Father Hyland of Dannemora prison." Then, he added, "The priest knew Wilder from when Hollywood came pitching a movie about the Father and his church at Dannemora, where your Uncle Fran had been imprisoned. And your uncle's friendship with the Father inspired the priest to introduce Wilder to Uncle Frankie. Instantly attracted to his charisma, Wilder hired him for the casting job."

Tony continued, "While shooting *The Seven-Year Itch*, Uncle Frankie told the director about the Cimino brothers' dramatic story. Billy knew their story was ripe for Hollywood, and he personally wanted to make the movie. Also, he was fixed on Uncle Frankie playing your uncle. As an actor, Uncle Frankie had the swagger to *be* your Uncle Fran, and he understood what motivated him throughout the family's decades of drama."

But Michael knew ultimately a movie about the Cimino brothers never got made, just like the failure to film the story of Father Hyland and his church. Still, he was curious about how the process played out with Wilder.

"What was Wilder's next move in trying to make this movie?" Michael asked. "After premiering *The Seven-Year Itch* and promoting Marilyn in a sexy outdoor stunt in New York City, Uncle Frankie and Billy visited your uncle. They came prepared with a storyboard to pitch, knocking on the door at Uncle Fran's Bath Beach home."

But why wasn't the movie made? Michael questioned while Tony was about to explain. "Wilder pitched the story to your uncle, and it was greater than any fiction. Seeing his life condensed into a storyboard amazed him. Your uncle wanted to authorize the film; he was impressed with Billy's passion and Uncle Frankie portraying him. But he was apprehensive about exposing his own family and negotiating with certain crime family bosses. After much consternation, your Aunt Isabella finally put the kibosh on it. She refused to relive the nightmare."

So, what might have been one of the great crime and redemption movies made for Hollywood never got made. Uncle Fran's decision to nix it was another testament that he was no longer living in the past. His period of adjustment had appeared to be over. He hoped.

TWENTY

Double-Double Cross

Although a movie about the Cimino brothers never happened, Michael became obsessed with his vision for a film. He wondered about driving the narrative, the story behind Lucky Luciano taking out his grandfather. Michael believed something big had put Jimmy Cimino in the middle of Luciano and his rise to the top of the Italian criminal organization. *So, what is it?*

The only living person who might be able to go back to the beginning and talk about it was Big Marcio. A skilled journalist, Michael was confident he could pry the backstory from him. He had learned from the older news pros how to get to the bottom of a story through the power of persuasion and relentless pursuit.

So, Michael contacted Big once again, focused and driven. He punched in his phone number and listened to the call going through, planning in his mind how to start the conversation. Big picked up the call, and Michael hesitated for a moment to get his opening just right.

"Hey, Big, it's Michael Cimino. I solved the mystery of Giuseppe Stefano! You suggested I figure it out on my own. Well, I did! He's the one who ate his *last meal* at Sing Sing. In fact, I recently spoke to his grandson, Tony Winston, who confirmed it indirectly, saying, 'the man met his destiny because he was born into a dangerous family.'"

"Good work!" Big said. "But I know you're calling to *ask* me about something else. Right?"

"Yes," replied Michael, maintaining a confident tone. "But first let me preface my question, Big. Bear with me, please. I already know Luciano ordered a hit on my grandfather. Uncle Fran had said as much in a letter he sent to my Aunt Isabella from Dannemora. Anyone in my family who knew this secret apparently had taken it to his or her grave. Of course, thanks to my Cousin James, who found and kept his grandfather's letters, I know it, too. But I must learn more, which triggered my phone call to you."

"So, you want to know what led up to the hit," Big guessed.

"That's right." Michael knew Big liked to talk. Playing to his ego, he added, "You're the only living person close to my family who may know the story behind the reported assassination of my grandfather. If you know what happened and then you die, the secret also dies with you. It'll be buried forever."

It seemed Michael had said the magic words. Big slowly began to spill the secret of his grandfather's apparent assassination. "During the year of the hit on your grandfather, you may know a war broke out many months earlier between rival gangsters from Manhattan and Brooklyn. This conflict became known as the Castellammarese War. The Masseria family, headed by Giuseppe 'Joe the Boss' Masseria, was based in Manhattan. And the rival Maranzano gang, run by Salvatore Maranzano, operated in Brooklyn."

Michael acknowledged to Big that he knew some

of the history, and he guessed that his grandfather may have been a casualty of this war. Michael recalled that his earlier research showed Masseria arrived in New York from Marsala, Sicily. And Maranzano came to New York from Castellammare del Golfo, Sicily (a little west of Palermo). Led by these respective bosses, the rival gangs seized each other's trucks, forced speakeasies around New York to use only Masseria's or Maranzano's products, and sabotaged each family's production and supply.

But there were details of the war that were not fully documented. "So, what came out of this gangland war?" Michael asked.

"Actually, the question should be *who* emerged? Among the shrewdest gang leaders who rose the ranks during the war was Lucky Luciano. He joined up with Meyer Lansky and Bugsy Siegel, both Jewish, and Frank Costello, who was originally from Calabria, Italy. All four men grew up together on the Lower East Side, and eventually they wanted to change the old Mafia traditions."

As for Luciano, Hollywood's depictions of him are sometimes fictionalized and conflicted. One commonality is that he's credited with creating the five New York crime families, which, over the decades, morphed into the Bonanno, Colombo, Gambino, Genovese, and Lucchese families.

But this is how Big Marcio characterized Luciano prior to organizing the five crime families, as told to him by Uncle Fran: Luciano and his three partners chose to work for Joe Masseria over Salvatore Maranzano. Still, the foursome was outgrowing

Sicilian lore and tiring of the bloodletting among rival gangsters. Led by Luciano, they were becoming more Americanized and set on changing the old Mafia structure. They were swayed by the corporate world of America, and Lansky was an accountant. He fit right into corporate thinking and was very influential.

"How did Luciano and his partners pursue their vision?" Michael asked.

"Luciano hatched a plan to pull off a double-double cross, arranging to have both Masseria and Maranzano killed so he could ascend to the top of both families. Luciano would first betray Masseria by telling Maranzano that he could lure Masseria to an Italian restaurant in Coney Island where he would be assassinated. And Luciano promised Maranzano that the boss of Brooklyn would then control Manhattan, along with his own territory."

"How did his plan turn into action?"

"In April of 1931, that restaurant became a crime scene as planned," Big continued. "Luciano, who was there, slipped into the men's room. Then a crew entered the restaurant and shot Masseria many times, slaughtering and killing him."

"So, who actually ordered the hit?" Michael asked. "Was Luciano or Maranzano responsible?"

Big then put an exclamation point on the climax to Michael's research. "Maranzano ordered it! Luciano was playing both ends against the middle. And who do you think he ordered to do the job?"

After delaying briefly to think it through, Michael finally said, "I don't know. However, I do know Uncle Fran spoke of regretting a job done for

Maranzano in 1931. He expressed his lament in another one of his letters sent home from Dannemora."

"Are you ready for this? asked Big, then pausing for impact. "Your grandfather and his two brothers did the hit! Maranzano had confidence in them and trusted them. They had ice water in their veins, and Leo was especially ruthless."

Michael, stunned and slow to react, then asked, "Are you serious?"

"Dead serious!"

All the pieces now started to fit together. And Michael conjured images of the three brothers performing the hit on Masseria. He imagined them walking into that restaurant—resolute, calculating and with nerves of steel like the steel guns in their hands. No fear! Michael now saw the brothers, his blood, as larger-than-life—overshadowing every hit man character in every mob movie ever made.

Removing Masseria changed the landscape of power. As Luciano promised, Maranzano would now control both Brooklyn and Manhattan, according to historical research which supported Big's statement. But Maranzano became suspicious of Luciano, and he had gotten wind that Lucky was plotting against him to take his place at the top.

So, Maranzano struck first, leaving Luciano severely cut up and for dead on Staten Island's South Beach. Miraculously, Luciano survived the hit, which is the reason he was nicknamed Lucky. That was Maranzano's mistake.

Michael and Big continued their conversation, as the former reporter focused on the final piece to the double-double cross. Michael reminded the man, who seemed to know everything, that he understood Maranzano's attempt to take out Luciano had failed. And his failure gave Lucky a chance to retaliate. Michael, as usual, had been thorough with his research, but any documented sources he reviewed did not provide all the details. "How did the hit on Maranzano go down?" he asked.

"Variations have surfaced over the years," said Big. "They range from Luciano and Lansky acting out the hit directly to a crew, posing as U.S. Treasury Department agents, doing the job ordered by the two partners. But this is how your Uncle Fran described what happened … Four imposters dressed as maintenance workers entered Maranzano's Brooklyn office to do their *dirty work*. Sent by Luciano and Lansky, they shot Maranzano and then stabbed him to death. By finishing Maranzano off with a knife, Lucky had sent his message of revenge for getting cut up—close to death—by Maranzano's crew."

Now Luciano had cleared his way to the top of organizational crime in New York City. He controlled Brooklyn and Manhattan and would soon create the five New York crime families and the Commission that governed them. But there was one person, known to have blind ambition of his own, still standing in his way.

That person would be Michael's grandfather, Vincenzo James. Again, Luciano made it clear to Uncle Fran that he had to remove Jimmy because the *number one* boss felt threatened by his ambition. Big said he'd heard about Luciano's admission directly from Uncle Fran. It reinforced what Michael had already known from reading Uncle Fran's letter.

~~~

Not everything can remain a secret forever. Secrets get exposed in the end, as history has shown. But one secret taken to the graves of several Cimino family members does appear buried for eternity: the aftermath of Vincenzo James's apparent murder.

TWENTY-ONE

No Stone Left Unturned
(Or None to be Found)

After Michael seemed to have solved the mystery leading to his grandfather getting gunned down, one stone remained unturned: What happened to his body?

Did Jimmy just disappear, never to turn up anywhere? Or was he legally buried in a cemetery, despite nobody in the Cimino family ever saying a word? Michael had never witnessed his father visiting the gravesite. And he was never made aware of a visit by anyone else either. Maybe his grandfather had been cremated, so there was no resting place for paying respect to his soul.

So, Michael's final internet quest was to find the information that documented his grandfather's death. After an exhausting search, he discovered a document that verified Vincenzo James's death, burial, and more.

The name on the document was James Cimino. For some reason, "Vincenzo" had been dropped. Perhaps because James was so commonly used by close friends and family members that he would be officially identified as *James* at death.

The document indicated he was born in Italy in 1905 and died from a gunshot wound that perforated his heart on December 1, 1931. It appeared to have confirmed what was reported by the *Brooklyn Daily*

Flyer so many years ago. And he was laid to rest in St. John's Cemetery in Middle Village, Queens, on December 5, 1931. There, he was with some very bad company. Many notorious crime bosses of the twentieth century were buried here—from Lucky Luciano to John Gotti and most of the New York mob kingpins in between them.

Jimmy's occupation was listed as marble cutter and setter. His father and mother: Giuseppe and Concetta Cimino. His wife and executor: Camila Cimino. The information about the family had lined up with its history and tree.

But Michael needed to contact the cemetery's property manager to reconfirm what he had just learned. After reaching out, all was reconfirmed, and he was given details of his grandfather's plot. Furthermore, Michael had learned from this property manager that the funeral home, which buried his grandfather, was still located in the old Gravesend neighborhood. But the funeral parlor would have no record of the burial going back that far to 1931.

Michael's next move was to visit his grandfather's gravesite. He needed that closure. So, in October of 2020, during the COVID-19 pandemic, he drove to St. John's Cemetery. Starting out, the day was sunny, but the moody skies turned increasingly dark gray as he got closer to the cemetery. Michael opened the car window and could smell the rain coming; he like the smell of rain. Still, it all was an ominous sign.

Driving along Woodhaven Boulevard to the main gates of the cemetery, Michael was amazed to see how the vast burial grounds extended for many blocks parallel to the road. To him, the grounds looked like a city of the dead, and he kept thinking about all the other big mob bosses who were buried there with his grandfather.

Michael arrived at the gates, and the anticipation of seeing his grandfather's gravestone was both eerie and exciting. Passing through the gates, it started to rain a little. He drove to St. John Cemetery's main office, which held records of the dead on a computer system in its basement. There, Michael got directions to the gravesite, and he mapped them out in his mind.

While walking to the plot, the rain became heavier. He had no umbrella but soldiered on his journey, raindrops dripping down the back of his neck, chilling him. And Michael thought about possibly being the only family member to visit the grave. It had seemed everyone in the family tried to live their lives forgetting about his grandfather. So many years had passed since the reported murder; so many family members had died or gone in different directions. For Michael, the first time in this cemetery visiting his grandfather's gravesite felt momentous, even life changing.

But trying to reach his destination took some time, and it was dizzying for him to see all the sections and rows running together. Not much distinguished them from each other. After locating the section, Michael began looking for Row U, which he tediously discovered and noted was marked by a tree with twisted branches that stood at the beginning of the row. He thought, with his typical sense of irony, *this tree seems symbolic of the Winston Family Tree, another strange signpost along the way.*

Now, Michael just had to find Jimmy's gravesite. At first glance, he missed seeing the headstone. Was he merely dizzied by all the sections, rows, and graves? That was what he believed, at first. But he soon learned there was a definite reason for not locating the gravestone—there was none! Between Grave 217 and 219, there was only empty space and hardened earth. He stared at the ground in disbelief. Michael so much wanted to see his grandfather's name on a stone at Grave 218 to validate him being buried here. But there was nothing. And he was disappointed that his journey—not just his trip to the cemetery, but all the time-consuming research building up to it—had ended this way. He felt dissatisfied, empty inside.

Was it possible that Jimmy had been buried in Grave 218, but the stone was removed for some unknown reason? Yes. Or maybe the family neglected to memorialize him with a gravestone. Odd that a family of stone and marble cutters and setters would not respect him by laying a stone in the ground. The only other resolution was this: Perhaps Vincenzo James Cimino was *not* buried in Grave 218, which explained Michael never hearing any talk of anyone visiting the gravesite. Thus, the burial was falsified—maybe an empty box was put in the ground.

Michael began believing his grandfather might have even survived the attack on his life. He remembered the phone call made to the old Coney Island Hospital to recover him. What if he had been recovered and resuscitated? Michael's imagination was so vivid now. He had mental images of the Cimino family secretly putting Jimmy on a boat in the night, going back to Italy, to hide him from another attempt on his life. *A fake burial and other diversions used by the street-smart family may have even fooled the savvy Luciano,* Michael fantasized. Uncle's Fran's letter from Dannemora prison alluded as much between the lines about Luciano's thinking—that Jimmy had been killed by Diamond Dick's gunshot (though he really might not have died at the time). Perchance Vincenzo James lived out his days high in the hills of Naples, far away from the madness. In this scenario, Jimmy did disappear—but alive! The trade-off would have been a bitter separation from his family at home, albeit several Ciminos and some of Concetta's people had remained in Naples.

Coming back to reality, Michael walked away from the gravesite, dejected. But he maintained some small hope of Jimmy's survival. Feeling a little numb now, he just stopped thinking. He drove home in the rain, only hearing the back-and-forth swishing of his windshield wipers. Focusing on the highway and white lines ahead helped him avoid dwelling on how it all had strangely ended earlier during the day.

After regrouping days later, he attempted to contact Big Marcio to find out if *he* had any answers to the graveyard enigma. He couldn't reach him. Sadly, Michael soon learned Big had died of the dreaded COVID-19 virus. Michael mourned Big, as the two men had grown close from their talks. Unable to rely on him anymore, there was no other family member alive to reveal the Cimino secrets of the past.

Sometimes mysteries refuse to be solved. So, Michael's compulsion about Jimmy's gravesite riddle would keep him forever wondering about the where-abouts of the man.

Still, it would not distract Michael from the work that remained. With research papers spread out on his desk, he stared at a blank computer screen. He took a long puff on his cigar, then blew out the smoke that lingered, and started to type, the keyboard clicking filled his ears, fueling him. Completing his first sentence about the Cimino brothers' saga, Michael knew for sure he had a story to tell, a legacy to document for future generations.

ABOUT THE AUTHOR

Gary M. Cianci, a former business journalist and public relations executive, lives with his wife, daughter, and dog in Brooklyn, New York. Writing the story to this novella had been a long-time dream. His career paths, encouraged by his parents, were a training ground for authoring the book.

The author welcomes communication and can be reached at marblestonepress@gmail.com.

Lightning Source UK Ltd.
Milton Keynes UK
UKHW020638141221
395640UK00012B/850

9 781737 987009